Dear Reader,

There is something about a man in uniform that gets me going. I know you understand what I'm talking about. But there's another side to that. Every time I see a man or woman in uniform, I think about the sacrifices they must go through and the fact that they face dangers most of us could never imagine. They put their lives on the line every day to protect us and to preserve democracy around the world.

Captain Will Hughes is a marine who's been through hell. The scars on the outside of his body are not the only ones that need to heal. When the fun-loving fashion designer Hannah Harrington steps into his life, he begins to wonder if there is more to life than the next mission.

Hannah has made it her mission to lighten Will's soul and to give him some comfort. What she doesn't expect are the many surprises that come with dating a marine.

I hope you love this couple as much as I do. I want to say a special thank-you to Kim, who helped me make sure my marine "stuff" was correct. Her husband is on active duty in a faraway land. I hope you'll email me at candacehavensbooks@gmail.com and tell me what you think of the book. You can also find me on Twitter/Facebook/MySpace through my website, www.candacehavens.com.

Enjoy!

Candace Havens

Candace Havens

MODEL MARINE

TORONTO NEW YORK LONDON
AMSTERDAM PARIS SYDNEY HAMBURG
STOCKHOLM ATHENS TOKYO MILAN MADRID
PRAGUE WARSAW BUDAPEST AUCKLAND

Recycling programs
for this product may
not exist in your area.

ISBN-13: 978-0-373-79650-2

MODEL MARINE

www.Harlequin.com

Printed in U.S.A.

ABOUT THE AUTHOR

Award-winning author and columnist Candace "Candy" Havens lives in Texas with her mostly understanding husband, two children and two dogs, Scoobie and Gizmo. Candy is a nationally syndicated entertainment columnist for FYI Television. She has interviewed just about everyone in Hollywood from George Clooney and Orlando Bloom to Nicole Kidman and Kate Beckinsale. You can hear Candy weekly on The Big 96.3 in the Dallas–Fort Worth Area. Her popular online writer's workshop has more than 1,300 students and provides free classes to professional and aspiring writers.

Books by Candace Havens

HARLEQUIN BLAZE
523—TAKE ME IF YOU DARE
607—SHE WHO DARES, WINS
613—TRUTH *AND* DARE

To all the servicemen and servicewomen, and their families, around the world. Thanks for all you do.

1

"THE MALE MODELS are in jail." Anne Marie whispered the words so Hannah wasn't sure if she heard her correctly. They were backstage working with the stylists to make sure the hair was correct for each model, and the deafening noise from the chatter made it difficult to converse without screaming. Anne Marie, the assistant director of Hannah Harrington Designs, had to be wrong. The fashion show launched in exactly forty-seven minutes and Hannah had planned everything down to the last stitch in the handbags the models would carry. There was no way something like this could happen.

Though it was freezing backstage, a small bead of sweat dampened her brow. "Did you say they're in jail?" Hannah tried to keep the panic from rising in her voice, but there was a tiny squeak at the end. "Oh, Anne Marie— You— No—take it back. I mean it. This is some kind of horrible joke. My entire life for the last six years is about to walk down that stage, and it has to be perfect. You know that. You promised me you had the models covered," she squeaked.

Anne Marie's lips formed a straight line at Hannah's harsh tone.

"Sorry." She'd been on edge the past few weeks and had lost her temper more than once. This was no time to make Annie Marie her whipping girl.

"Don't you dare apologize, Hannah. I know I screwed up." Anne Marie's jaw jutted out and her hands were in fists. "I saw them at Jake's party last night and they were drinking. I should have sent them home then. This sucks, and I've totally failed you. I just don't know how to fix it in—" Anne Marie glanced at her watch "—forty-three minutes."

Hannah glanced around the tent, searching for any man who could fill out the jeans she'd designed. It had been a risky venture to do male and female lines in her first collection, but it had paid off. Before tonight's show she had received great buzz in the fashion world from some of the magazine editors who'd toured her collection early. Without the men, the show wouldn't work. They were her big reveal.

The only men in a sea of six-foot female models were the ones doing hair, and they were all too short, pasty and waif-thin.

Are there any real men left in Manhattan?

She closed her eyes and lifted her head in a silent prayer.

I'm going to walk out the door, and I'm going to find two of the most handsome men I've ever seen in my life who will fit perfectly into my show.

Yeah, right.

Opening her eyes again she headed out.

"Where are you going?" Anne Marie cried.

"To find the men of my dreams," Hannah said determinedly. "Check and make sure the girls have their belts right-side up, and that Clara wears the pink cowboy boots. I'll be back in ten minutes."

Hannah had almost convinced herself she would find the men she needed just outside the tent, or in the crowd waiting to get in. No such luck.

The good news was there was a crowd.

The bad news was that ninety-nine percent of it was women.

Any men she saw were either way too short, or a little thick around the middle. She never cared about anyone's size, but she needed a perfect fit for the jeans. Worried she might be recognized, Hannah pulled her cowboy hat down low on her eyes, and made her way around the crowd and out onto Columbus.

Shivering against the cold, she pulled her leather jacket tighter, which did nothing for her legs, which were in tights and a miniskirt.

As usual on Friday afternoon, the area was packed with people. There were some teens in baggy jeans and shirts, but they were all either too skinny or too short to fit in the clothes.

She didn't want to think about the worst-case scenario, but she had to.

Please. I haven't come this far to fail.

Everything she had was tied up in this show. If the editors hadn't had a sneak peak she could get away with losing the final two, but that was what most of the buzz had been about.

Glancing down at her watch she grimaced. Only thirty-two minutes till go-time. Tears brimmed her eyes. She tried to blink them back, but one errant drop of water slid down her cheek. She shoved it away with the heel of her hand.

This is no time to cave. Get it together.

"Whoever he is, he isn't worth that tear," a deep, whiskey-toned voice said from beside her.

Hannah lifted her head and met a pair of the most beautiful green eyes she'd ever seen on a man. Then she stepped back—stunned—to find the perfect male specimen attached to those eyes. His blond hair was cut short, his shoulders broad, and, dressed in his blues, he was the sexiest man she'd ever seen.

She had to remind herself to breathe.

"Hello, Marine."

"Ma'am." He tipped his hat.

This couldn't be happening. She glanced down to his hips and then up to his face. He was absolutely beautiful. But there was also something about him. A presence, something that symbolized a strength that had nothing to do with the uniform he wore.

He smiled, seemingly amused by her appraisal.

"Hmm." She tapped her finger against her chin and then grinned. "How do you feel about helping a damsel in distress?"

"It's what I do, ma'am. Did he hurt you? I can't stand a man beating on a woman. That's one of the things that sends my temper over the edge, and I have to warn you I do have one."

Charmed by his slight Southern accent, she'd lost what he was saying. "You have one what?"

"A temper."

"Oh, no. This isn't about a man. But I need you like no woman has ever needed you. In fact, my life depends on you coming with me right now. And you would make me the happiest woman in the world if you had a friend who is just as hot as you."

The marine put two fingers in his mouth and whistled.

Hannah jumped slightly at the piercing volume.

There was a thud of running footsteps, and another man, this one with dark hair and light caramel skin, joined them. He stopped in front of the other marine, his hand flying up to a salute.

"You whistled, Captain, sir." His voice was clipped, but respectful. Hannah didn't know her marine ranks very well, but she knew that a captain was up there. She was crazy to ask these men to help her, but she didn't have much of a choice.

"Lieutenant, seems we have a damsel in distress."

The marine glanced down at Hannah, his dark eyes checking her face for injuries. "Are you hurt?"

She smiled brightly. "No, but I need your help. Can you gentlemen follow me? I promise, if you give me the next hour of your life, you'll save mine. And I'll throw in the best meal you've ever had."

She reached out her hands and wriggled her fingers, begging them to follow.

Both men shrugged.

"Captain, sir, if there's food involved, I'm in."

"Then let's get to it." The captain took Hannah's hand. "Fair damsel, lead the way," he said.

Hannah didn't have time to question her good fortune, or the fact that the marine warmed her with his touch. She had a show to put on and a career to save. With these two, she had a feeling she was going to kill Lincoln Center in a way that had never been done before.

CAPTAIN WILL HUGHES had done dumb things in his life, especially when it came to women, but this would go to the top of his crazy list. In the past fifteen minutes he'd been asked to strip, put on a pair of great-fitting jeans and a shirt that forced him to keep his arms by his sides, and while one woman messed with the shirt, another held out a pair of cowboy boots for him to slip on.

"His chest is too damn big," the woman said through the pins in her mouth. "I've never seen so many muscles in my life. Hannah, what do you want me to do?"

Hannah stood there appraising him for a few seconds. The desire in her eyes made his crotch uncomfortable. It had been too damn long for him, and she was his idea of the perfect woman. From that honey-blond hair piled on top of her head in a mass of curls, to her pert breasts, down to long legs ending in red cowboy boots she was nothing short of gorgeous. Surrounded by models, none compared to her beauty.

"Leave the shirt open. Though, they probably won't

be looking at the clothes when he walks out." Hannah laughed, and something tugged at Will's heart.

"One minute. Line up, people!" someone screeched.

The tension in the room was palpable and the noisy din died down.

"What's wrong?" Will glanced around the tent to see what was happening.

"Nothing. Show's about to begin and we need it quiet back here so everyone can hear their cues." Hannah waved over Rafael. As the models walked by, it looked as if his friend was watching a tennis match. Rafe always had a way with women. "All I need you guys to do is walk at a steady pace to the end of the stage, pause about fifteen seconds and walk back. You need to be prepared for the photographers' flashes when you pause. It can be blinding at times.

"Just give them your best marine glare. You can watch what the girls do on that screen right there." She pointed to a flat-screen television. "Kayleigh is the stage manager and she'll tell you when to go on. You'll enter here, and exit the stage on the other side. I can't thank you guys enough. And I'll owe you big if we can just get through the next twenty minutes."

He was a marine, and would have helped her no matter what, but Will liked the fact she felt she owed him. He could think of at least thirty different ways she could pay him back.

Mind out of the gutter, Marine.

"We've got it covered," Will told her.

"That's right," Rafe said. "If there's one thing marines can do, it's follow orders."

"You guys really are the best." She squeezed Will's arm. Then she left to take her position near the other side of the stage.

"Sir, we've been in some tough situations, but I never thought I'd have to be a male model," Rafe whispered. "Promise me none of the guys will ever hear about this. Otherwise we'll never live it down. Though, I got to admit, I love these damn jeans."

Will chuckled. "Mine could be a size bigger, but I like them, too. And trust me, no one will ever hear a word out of me. I appreciate you helping out."

Rafael shrugged. "It's what we do."

"Showtime!" The stage manager waved her hand.

"Sir?"

"Yeah, Rafe?"

"Are you nervous?"

"We're marines. We don't have nerves." He winked at the man. "But if I did, I'd tell you I'd rather be in the desert fighting hostiles than walking out on that stage."

"Me, too, sir. Me, too."

Poor guy. They'd been looking forward to doing some sightseeing before they had to report to the UN the next day as part of a defense attaché force. It would be Will's job to coordinate the teams assigned to protect foreign dignitaries for a global conference in town. Most of the preliminary work had been done, so he and Rafe had been kicking around the past twenty-four hours as tourists.

"You're up!" A woman touched his arm and gently shoved him forward. Will hadn't even noticed he'd advanced to the stage. He swallowed and walked up the few steps. He saw Rafe exit the other side, and the stage manager told him to go.

The lights blinded him as he stepped out onto the white-carpeted floor and walked to what he hoped was the end. He couldn't really see until he damn near fell off the thing. He stood there for a moment while the cameras flashed, but couldn't figure out why everyone was screaming. People were up on their feet clapping. He turned and walked back, forcing himself not to run.

"Holy crap! They've gone ape out there." Hannah was there to guide him off the stage. "You two were amazing." She stood on her tiptoes and kissed Will full on the mouth. He wanted it to last longer, but then she moved on to Rafe. The other man received a hug, but not a kiss. That sat just fine with Will.

She took them both by the hands. "Okay, you two, one more time down and back and we are done."

"Again?" he and Rafe said at the same time.

Laughing, she pulled them up the steps and onto the stage.

The lights were different this time and he could see more of the audience. They were giving Hannah a standing ovation. He had no right to be proud of her, but he was. He held up her hand as if she'd won a prize-fight. They walked that way to the end of the stage and back.

He helped her down the steps and then she wrapped her arms around his neck.

"Marine, I have to do some press for a bit, and then we can do anything you want. You name it!" She gave him another quick peck and she was off.

"Why do I have the feeling you're going to tell me to get lost?" Rafe chuckled behind him.

"As soon as I find my pants you're getting a hundred bucks, and I'm giving you the night off to see the city," Will told him.

"That's all right, sir. I think I might be kind of busy, too." Rafe winked at a model with short pixie hair and blue eyes. She blew him a kiss with her fingers.

"Guess this modeling thing isn't so bad after all." Will chuckled.

And the woman of his dreams had promised him anything.

Luckily he knew exactly what he wanted.

2

A DREAMLIKE TRANCE enveloped Hannah in a shroud of happiness.

Success.

The thrill of it pulsed through her veins. For more than an hour and a half one reporter after another interviewed her, and she'd been air-kissed and hugged by hundreds of people she didn't know.

"I'm sorry, we have appointments to keep this evening. Thank you for coming," Anne Marie said as she pulled her from the media frenzy.

"That was—"

"Freakin' stellar." Anne Marie hugged her.

"We did it." Hannah squeezed her friend tight.

Kayleigh squealed behind them. "Who knew we would be the hottest thing at Fashion Week? And hello! I just checked the machine at the office, and we have tons o' calls from buyers and editors." Kayleigh was a terrific publicist and stage manager. She helped Anne

Marie hire the models, and even designed the look of the show within the parameters Hannah had given her.

They gathered hands and did a happy dance they'd made up when they discovered Hannah's designs had been chosen for this special New Stars of Fashion event.

"Why is it you leave me out of everything?" Jesse, her fabric guru, mumbled. They opened their arms to him.

"Group hug," Anne Marie ordered. Hannah and the others complied.

"Tonight wouldn't have happened without you guys," Hannah stated matter-of-factly.

"Phfft," Jesse said. "You have more talent than the majority of designers at Fashion Week combined. You would have succeeded no matter what."

She kissed his cheek. "No, I wouldn't have. You guys kept me sane. Each of you is so important I can't even—" Emotion clogged her throat so she cleared it.

"If you cry, I will hit you," Anne Marie warned. She was a tough one. Dressed in her requisite fishnets, black mini and vintage rocker T-shirt, she knew her friend would follow through with the threat.

"No tears. Just gratitude for some really great friends."

Someone moved just outside the circle and she saw the handsome marine who had saved her show.

"Hey!" She waved to Will.

He nodded.

"I promised to take him to dinner so I'll see you guys later. Thank you again."

"Wait," Anne Marie yelled. "Don't forget you have

Leland's party at seven. He's throwing it for you, so you have to be there. We'll get everything packed and meet at Leland's."

Hannah had forgotten. She glanced at Will and then at Anne Marie. She didn't want to disappoint Will, but she owed Leland so much. It would be selfish to bail on a party in her honor. "I'll be there."

Will waited for her near the entrance.

"I thought you would have given up on me, but I'm glad you didn't." She suddenly felt shy. After seeing him without a shirt, she'd wanted him in the most carnal of ways. But she also had an enormous respect for him. What he had done for her couldn't have been easy for him or his friend.

And they had saved her show. Will and Rafe were two of the biggest reasons people were excited about her clothes.

Who could blame them?

Captain Will Hughes was walking sex. That seriously hot uniform he wore hid the rippling muscles, but she'd seen the goods and she couldn't stop thinking about them. Hannah clasped her hands behind her back so she wouldn't touch him again.

"You asked me to wait, and I'm good at taking orders."

She smiled at that. "I would have thought a captain was used to giving them."

"I do my fair share of that, too, but I'm a marine and there is always someone barking orders somewhere higher up."

Feeling lucky that she didn't have to deal with anyone, except an occasionally cranky Anne Marie, she patted his arm. She hoped the contact would calm her nerves. No dice.

"Congratulations. From what I understand you had a great night. I don't know much about fashion, but those reporters seemed to like what you did."

Uncomfortable with the praise from him, Hannah bent her head and stared at her toes. "They liked you and your friend, Rafe. You guys sold the show. Where is he?" She glanced around.

Will motioned with his thumb toward the entrance. "He left about fifteen minutes ago with one of the models."

"That doesn't surprise me. All the girls were talking about you guys. I really can't thank you enough."

"It's not a big deal. So are you ready to go?"

Hannah scrunched her face. "I am, but there's one thing I have to do. I forgot my friend Leland is throwing a big party in my honor. We don't have to stay long, but I must make an appearance. He's invited a lot of industry peeps and—"

Will grinned. "I get it. Do you want to take a rain check on the dinner?"

"No. That is, if you don't. I'd really like you to be my, uh…" She couldn't get the words out.

"Date?" His face was a mask and she had no idea what he was thinking.

She nodded.

"I'd be honored. But won't your friend—" he pointed toward Jesse "—mind? You guys seem close."

"Jesse?" She coughed back the laughter. "Uh, no. He works for me. We call him the intern, but as you can see he's not very internish looking. He's been helping me with fabrics and pattern-making. Genius, that guy. But not interested in me in the least. And I have nothing but sisterly feelings for him. I think he might have something for my friend Anne Marie, but they're both so busy neither of them have noticed yet. Look at me, Miss Gossip. Sorry. The answer is *no*. I am thoroughly unattached."

He smiled the warmest smile she'd ever seen.

Without thinking she threw herself at him and kissed his cheek. "Oh, sorry. It's just you look so sweet. I'm, uh, overexcited tonight."

"Don't apologize. Trust me." His husky voice deepened.

The heat of his words spread through her like a match to tinder.

"In casual circumstances I'd rather not wear my uniform. Do I have time to go back to my hotel and change?"

Her first instinct was to offer him something from her collection but she remembered how tight the shirts were. If he went to Leland's party with his chest bared the females and males would maul him before he could get through the door. Her heart did double-time as she remembered how he looked strutting down the runway with his tough-guy 'tude.

"Sure."

"Let's get out of here and grab a taxi."

IN GREENWICH VILLAGE, the festivities were in full swing. When they entered Leland's penthouse everyone yelled, "We love you, Hannah."

Her hand flew to her chest and her eyes burned with tears. But she refused to let them fall because she was so happy so many of her friends were there. She grabbed Will's hand and pulled him into the throng.

"Darling girl, you were fabulous tonight. And your Adonis was the perfect touch," Leland said as he air-kissed both of her cheeks.

"Thank you for this."

"Who would have thought that frizzy-haired girl who begged to work as a seamstress would turn out to be the It Girl of the fashion world?"

She smiled. "You did. From that first day you seemed to see something in me that even I didn't know I had."

He chucked her under the chin. "Talent, love. It was oozing out of every pore. Now introduce me to the Adonis."

Will stuck out his hand. "I'm Will. It's nice to meet you. So you gave Hannah her first big break?"

"I did indeed. And how did you two meet?" Leland was a lot of things, but he was never subtle.

"Uh…" Hannah stammered. Her first instinct was to lie because she didn't want to embarrass Will. But her brain stalled.

"She kidnapped me off the street and made me do her bidding," Will interjected.

Leland guffawed. "That sounds like my Hannah. When she finds what she wants, she's like a little terrier. She never lets go. It's nice to meet you, Will. I hope you enjoy the party, you two. Simply *everyone* is here."

They spent the next half hour greeting the guests—a delicious selection of Manhattan's weird and wonderful. Will hadn't even flinched when Brandy, who was really cross-dressing Randy, fingered the collar of his button-down shirt. She couldn't blame Randy. More than once she found herself brushing up against Will just to feel those hard muscles underneath.

They finally made it over to Anne Marie and the gang. "I wanted to officially introduce you to the people who are really responsible for the great show tonight. This is Anne Marie, our assistant director of design. She keeps me on track and pretty much runs the business side of things."

"Pretty much?" Anne Marie snorted.

"True. She runs the business."

Hannah pointed to her other favorite person in the world. "Kayleigh handles all the press, along with Anne Marie. She's a publicist who does a million other things, as well. She was the stage manager giving the orders tonight."

"My bark is worse than my bite." Kayleigh winked.

"Ha! Don't scare poor Will away," Hannah playfully admonished.

"The captain doesn't look like he scares easily," Kayleigh said suggestively.

Will shook his head.

Hannah chose to ignore the flirting. She knew Kayleigh was just giving her a hard time.

"And this guy is Jesse." Her friend stuck out his hand to shake Will's. "He answered the ad for an intern eight months ago, and none of us are sure how we lived without him before that. He has forgotten more about fabrics and textiles than I will ever know. And he's a mean pattern maker. I've never met anyone better."

"She likes to make us sound good," Jesse countered. "And the reason we're all here is because she's got an imagination bar none, and she is a design genius."

Hannah made an unladylike noise. "That is so not true. Now who's being over the top? Trust me, none of this would work without the whole gang. I can be a tyrant at times, but they put up with me."

She noticed no one came to her defense about the tyrant remark. They obviously hadn't forgotten her numerous breakdowns over the past few weeks. She tried not to let the pressure get to her, but she didn't always succeed.

"It's great to meet you," Will said to her team. "I don't know much about this world. In truth, I don't know anything, but I've been listening in on conversations all night. Everyone seems excited about the show."

"Thanks," the three said in unison.

"You better get back out there and circulate. Your fans await," Anne Marie encouraged her.

"Hannnaaah." Larisa Malone always elongated her name. The shrill voice sent a painful sting through Hannah's chest. Dressed in leather from head to toe, false eyelashes and garish red lipstick, the other woman looked more like a drag queen than Randy did. "You are quite the surprise, aren't you? How does it feel?" The words might sound like a compliment but the tone was vicious.

Hannah poked Anne Marie when she noticed a sneer on the woman's face.

"Oh, Larisa, tomorrow morning they'll be on to someone else. Are you ready for your show on Thursday?"

"Of course. I have quite a few surprises up my sleeves."

She glanced over Hannah's shoulder and waved. "Oh, my, that's Justin T. I was *so* surprised to see him at your little show. He usually only makes an appearance for the great designers. I must tell him how delicious he was in that last movie he made."

"That one is a piece of work." Will scratched his head as Larisa left. "She reminds me of the women who play bridge with my mother. None of them ever has a kind word about another person and they also have sticks up their— Oh, sorry."

Hannah smiled. "Oh, don't be. You have her pegged. And as a result, you're my new hero."

Before Will could answer, Christopher Kline appeared. "Doll, great show." He was Leland's lover and one of the most influential chefs in New York City. Every restaurant he owned turned to gold.

She hugged him. "Thank you."

He glanced up at Will and gave him a once-over. "Leland didn't lie. You did find yourself a *real* man."

She teased him back. "Behave."

He waggled his eyebrows. "That is not how I roll, Hannah, love. Oh, and did you hear the gossip from the Hags in the corner? Such jealousy about you, the hate spews like a river of lies. That means you are on top, my sweet. Leland says you killed, so watch out for the claws."

Hannah peered over his shoulder. The Hags, as everyone called them, were three women who had tried to design their own lines, only to fall flat on their faces. So instead of going back to the drawing board, they became online fashion critics. Their site didn't have a single nice review but they had a huge following. Unfortunately, people seemed to eat up their wickedness. They wore too much makeup and their clothes were meant for women twenty years their junior. Hence, their name.

"I guess it would be too much to hope they'd give me a pass."

"My darling Hannah, sometimes your naïveté brings such a lightness to my cold, dead heart. Don't worry. You know how it works. The more they hate you, the more everyone else will love you."

"I suppose," she grumbled.

"Now you two run off and get some food. Leave those sorry wannabes to me. I have a bit of juicy gossip that might just lead them off your scent."

Before he left, he blew her a kiss and nodded to Will.

Will guided her to the dining area that had been set up banquet style. "I didn't realize the fashion business was so cutthroat," he said.

"It's the worst, really. I'm lucky Leland invited a lot of my friends, too, who are really sweet. But he has to include some of the others because to snub them is a big faux pas."

"I always feel sorry for people like those women and the one who came up to you before. They obviously have no self-esteem if they have to beat up on others to make themselves feel better. They are no better than the bullies on the playground."

She stood on her tiptoes to kiss him on the cheek again. "You really are my hero."

"Let's go eat," he said, changing the subject. He seemed to be uncomfortable whenever she tried to compliment him. "I don't know about you, but that modeling is hard work."

They stood in front of the food table and she was surprised when Will ate a big plate of sushi.

He caught her watching him.

"What?"

"I'm sorry. I seem to have all these misconceptions about marines. I assumed you were more of a meat-and-potatoes kind of guy."

He shrugged. "I've been stationed all over the world, and I've learned to eat whatever is available. And honestly, most anything is better than what you get in the mess hall. Or my mom's cooking. I love her, but she has never belonged in a kitchen. As for the meat and potatoes, I never turn down a good steak."

"Well, I'm one of those crazies who is allergic to wheat, white rice, shellfish and dairy," Hannah admitted. She loved food, but had learned long ago that her body had specific needs. Her allergic reactions varied from rashes to her throat swelling so badly she couldn't breathe. "So I eat a lot of protein and vegetables and fruit. None of which are here." The table was laden with sushi, dim sum and all types of puff pastries filled with a variety of meats and shrimp.

Will put his chopsticks down. "Do you want to get

out of here and find something else to eat? Is that okay, since it's your party?"

She was starving and alone time with Will didn't seem like such a bad idea. The crazy day and several nights of no sleep sent her into zombie mode. She wasn't sure how much longer she could hold up the pretense. "The bathroom is near the entrance—if anyone asks, that's where we are headed."

"Yes, ma'am." He covered her hand in his and pulled her through the crowd.

A few seconds later they were out in the hallway with hopefully no one the wiser. "That was much easier than I thought it would be." Hannah's shoulders dropped about an inch.

Will laughed. "I caught a few people staring and whispering. They're probably thinking the worst."

Hannah grabbed a clip from her purse and put her hair back up in a loose ponytail. She was already more relaxed now that she didn't have to impress the denizens of the fashion world. "My guess is they're jealous. How would you feel about a steak?"

"Like I said, I never turn one down."

AFTER THEIR MEAL at the steak house, Will escorted Hannah to her studio. It was only a few blocks away and she wanted to walk off the calories she'd eaten. As far as he could see, her body was perfect. Every time she brushed against him at the party he had to control his libido.

She'd warned him, been so worried about how he would view her friends. They were definitely eccentric, but many of them were good people. Will's instincts when it came to judging people had never steered him wrong. Besides, she should hang out with a group of marines on a Friday night. That was some weirdness.

"You suddenly seem really far away," Hannah said.

He squeezed her hand. "I'm right here."

"I'm not sure I'll ever be able to thank you for everything you've done today."

"Hannah, I told you earlier. I was happy to help. And tonight, well, I've had a great time."

"Me, too." She smiled up at him sweetly.

That grin was a like a light directed straight to his blackened soul. There were times the past two years when he wondered if he would ever feel joy again. Throughout dinner he found himself relaxing and even laughing at times. Hannah did that to him and he feared he could become addicted to her quite easily.

She stopped in front of a five-story building. "This is me. It's been a long day, but I was wondering if you would come upstairs. There's something I want to give you."

He paused as he tried to figure out what she meant.

"Uh, that sounded so lurid. I promise I have no— uh, you know, on your body…uh. Yeah. Do you want to come up?"

"Sure. It's hard to say *no* to an invitation like that." Though Will had to admit, he wished she did have designs on his body. At the very least he wanted to deeply explore the kiss they shared earlier in the night.

Inside the building he was surprised to see her name

across a door on the first floor, but she led him to a freight elevator.

"That's my studio. I rent out the rest of the floors as loft spaces. We have a cool view of the Hudson on the back side of the building."

"You own the building?"

She smiled. "I inherited it from my grandmother, along with an apartment on the Upper West Side. I sublet that one, too. I like being close to work because I never know when a creative binge is going to happen so I moved into the penthouse here. Plus, I'm not really a west-sider. My parents are, but not me."

Will knew enough about Manhattan real estate to understand that was a pricey neighborhood. She must have come from a wealthy family.

"Were they at your show tonight?"

"Who?" The elevator opened and they entered her apartment. Everything was white and she hadn't lied about the view. The lights flickered across the river.

"Your parents. Were they at your event this afternoon?"

She laughed, but it wasn't a happy sound. "My parents are mortified by my choice of profession."

Will was surprised. "You can't be serious. I thought people with money like that loved clothes."

She dumped her bag on a coffee table in front of a long sectional couch. Except for a giant flat-screen hanging on the wall it was the only thing in this part of the loft. He could see a filmy curtain in the back that separated her bedroom from the rest of the area.

A fridge and a microwave were the only appliances in the kitchen.

How does she cook a meal without an oven or a stovetop?

Will didn't have a home, except for his parents' house. Financially, it made no sense to have a place of his own—he was in the U.S. Marine Corps and he lived wherever they sent him. He never accumulated much in the way of belongings because of his travels. But Hannah hadn't seemed one to like a sparse lifestyle. The clothing at her show was colorful and fun. He wasn't sure what he expected but it wasn't this.

"Most of them do love clothing. My family is from old money. My mother has a stylist who buys everything she wears. I'm not sure she's ever stepped foot in a department store or even a boutique. The clothes and the jewels all come to her. And my dad, well, he lives to work. My mother has all of his clothes made by the same tailors who seamed my grandfather's clothing."

Slipping off her heels, she tossed them on the floor near the bar in her kitchen.

He stifled the urge to pick them up and put them where they were supposed to go. Will had a thing about order. Rafe called him OCD, but his friend wasn't much better. Most of the marines he knew liked to keep their belongings tidy. It was a part of the lifestyle. They never knew when they'd be called into action.

"Wow! Talking about my parents just sucked the life right out of the room." She motioned to the couch. "Go have a seat. I'll be back in a minute."

While it was only ten-thirty, Will had dated enough

to know a minute to a woman was often a half hour in man time. He flipped on the television and turned the volume down low. He watched the end of the news and then switched to see a documentary on the National Geographic channel.

"Oh, I love that movie, except for that poor wilde-beest who doesn't see the lion coming."

Will turned to see her in drawstring pajama bottoms and a long-sleeve T-shirt. Her hair had been pulled up into a fluffy ponytail. He liked that she was comfort-able enough around him that she probably would have dressed the same as if he weren't here. Though, if she was trying to seduce him she was doing a great job. Her natural beauty was like lightning striking his body with pure heat.

If she were trying to seduce you, she would have worn something sexier.

She handed him something soft.

"It's a scarf. I made it for my brother, Tyler, for Christmas. But I noticed you didn't have one and it's supposed to get really cold the next few days."

Will unraveled the scarf. It was tightly woven, but incredibly soft. "What about your brother?"

She sat down on the L of her couch next to him. "I have several months to make him a new one."

"Thank you. It's beautiful and that you made it makes it even more special."

Her smile lit up her face and he could feel that light sear through his heart.

"I wanted you to have it. I like the idea of you having a part of me wrapped around you." Her hand flew to her mouth. "I can't believe that came out the way it did. I meant since you were so incredible today... I give up." She covered her face and shook her head.

Will's heart felt as though it beat double-time as he reached up and pulled her hands away from her face.

"You never have to be embarrassed with me." He touched her cheek gently with the back of his fingers. Her skin was so smooth. It took all of his resolve to keep from hauling her into his lap. "I should get going." Those words were tough to say but he was doing his best to be a gentleman.

Her lips formed a straight line. "I forgot you have a job to go to tomorrow morning." She touched his hand. "I've kept you out late and—"

"Hannah, stop. It's only eleven and I do want to stay. Trust me I do. But you've had a really long and eventful day. I saw you hiding the yawns during dinner."

"Oh, no, and here I thought I was being so clever with my napkin. I haven't slept for a couple of days. So much was riding on this show. But, and I know how this makes me sound, I don't want to be alone. Can you stay, just for a little while? We can watch the documentary and I have popcorn and beer or wine. And maybe some cheese and bottled water. I eat out a lot."

"I figured as much when I saw your kitchen. I'm happy to stay if you aren't too tired."

"Stay right there."

She ran off to the kitchen and returned with some beer and a giant bowl of popcorn. She scooted in next to him and he slipped his arm across her petite shoulders.

Less than ten minutes later Will had to save her

couch by grabbing the bottle of beer out of her hand. She'd fallen asleep.

When he shifted to put the bowl of popcorn on the coffee table, she fell into his lap. He grabbed a pillow to put between her and his thighs, praying that she didn't feel the sudden bulge when she'd touched him there.

Will pushed the tiny tendrils that escaped her ponytail away from her face. She was the most beautiful woman he'd ever seen.

Now what the hell am I going to do?

3

HANNAH OPENED HER EYES to find the television was on. She yawned and noticed she was lying on her sofa pillow, which was on top of two strong thighs.

Will.

Great. I fell asleep.

Turning her head, she glanced up to find an amused look on his face.

"Hey." That whiskey voice got to her every time.

She sat up and tugged the pillow from his lap. "Okay, I'm mortified. I can't believe I did that."

"You had a good excuse." He stood and stretched. His shirt lifted enough she caught a glimpse of his hardened abs. The lower region of her body reacted instantly. "You were right about the documentary. It was great."

His next words would be about him needing to leave. He'd be polite and obliging but she wasn't ready for that yet. The man was so handsome that part of her wondered if he was a hallucination. If he were a dream, she would make the most of it.

"Will? I don't ask men I just met to stay overnight."

"I was heading out." He was so earnest.

Hannah made a bold move without even thinking about it. She quickly stood before him and placed her hand on his chest.

"Um, you misunderstood. What would you think of me if I told you I want you to stay? That I want to do naughty, dirty things to your body. That I—"

Before she could say another word his lips captured hers, his tongue begging for entrance as it teased her lips. With the lightest touch his knuckle outlined her jaw.

Her hands lifted his shirt so she could run her palms up and down the muscles beneath.

Will moaned when she touched him and he twined her hands up around his neck so that her body was flush against his, her breasts rubbing against his hard chest. There was a strange sense of coming home, almost as if she could feel her body binding to his.

His hand moved behind her head and he loosened her ponytail. "Your hair is like wavy sunshine."

Her hair was her arch enemy but now wasn't the time to talk about that.

When she glanced up, the need in his eyes stole her breath. He wanted her as much as she did him.

"Hannah, are you trying to seduce me?"

"If you think I'm just trying, then I'm obviously not doing it very well. I'll race you to the bedroom," she said as she took off in a dead run, sliding across the floor in her socks.

"Hey, you cheated."

"It's only cheating if there are rules and there are no rules tonight, Will." She slipped off her clothes and he did the same. A few seconds later, they watched each other from opposite sides of the bed. Naked. His cock was at attention and Hannah wondered at the length and width of him.

A slight panic engulfed her. He was so big.

Before she could think too much about it, she climbed on the bed and sat on her knees in the middle of it. Will mirrored her. Even in the dark, she could see two circular scars below his right shoulder. There were also burn marks on his left shoulder. The pink tissue was tight and angry-looking. With one finger she touched him lightly.

"What happened?"

"Bomb and sniper in Baghdad." The pain in those words struck her. Though somehow she knew he didn't want her sympathy.

She couldn't imagine everything he'd been through. The horrors he had seen and the pain he must have experienced with his injuries. Her every instinct wanted to protect him from harm, to soothe his pain.

"Hannah?" Will was watching her carefully.

She would have to work harder to hide her emotions from him.

"You know I'm just using you for your body, right?"

He chuckled. "You don't see me complaining."

She had a feeling he didn't do much smiling and if she could bring a little lightness to his world, well…

His hand slid down her arm.

She took his hand and put it on her breast over her

heart and wondered if he could feel the speed of the beating there. His thumb grazed the nipple, causing it to harden. When he replaced his thumb with his tongue, Hannah sucked in a breath.

Still sitting on her knees she arched back and cried out when his teeth gently nipped her. Continuing to tease her, his hands went to work on the rest of her body, eventually inching down to her heat.

Her breath coming in tiny pants, Hannah separated her knees to give him access. She needed him to touch her there, to relieve the tension building in her body.

He didn't disappoint. He turned her so that her back was too him and her butt on his thighs. The length of him was underneath her cheeks. He rubbed her sensitive nub with extraordinary speed and pressure.

"Yes," she cried as he brought her to orgasm.

"Will," she screamed. He didn't let go. Three more times he brought her to the peak until her body was hot liquid.

Once again he shifted her so that she faced him. Hannah lifted herself and slipped his cock inside her. His deep moan caused a flurry of excitement. She bounced up and down, riding him hard. He met her thrust for thrust. Hannah threw her head back as Will sucked in a nipple. Every time his tongue rasped against her, there was the feeling she was becoming unglued. Her body shuddered with another orgasm and her heat tightened around him.

"Hannah," he moaned as he pounded her even faster and then released his seed.

His arms tightened around her and they kissed, both of their bodies shuddering with tremors.

This man was everything.

"That was—"

He kissed her again. "Yeah. It was," he said as he nuzzled her neck.

Hannah was spent and happier than she'd been in a really long time.

There were lovers in her past. She'd even had great sex. Well, she'd thought it was great until tonight. Will had taken her to a whole new level. A cool February draft from the windows sent goose bumps down her arms and legs.

"You're cold. Let's get you under the covers."

"I'm fine," she protested, not wanting to move just yet.

His hands cradled her face. "You're cold. I can feel you shivering." He lifted her off him and then pulled the sheets and comforter back on his side of the bed. They slid into the pocket he made and she had to admit this was better.

As he warmed her against his chest, she smiled.

"This part is always kind of awkward." She laughed.

"Why do you say that?"

She lifted her head so she could see his face. "I don't know. You've just made crazy, carnal jungle love, losing all inhibitions, and then, it's over. Everything is quiet and you're searching for something to talk about."

Hannah wished she hadn't said it, but her mouth was always jumping ahead of her brain.

Will tugged her hair gently. "Well, if you give me

about five minutes we can get straight back to that—
what did you call it? Carnal jungle love?"

"Five minutes? Really? Wow. What are we going to
do until then?"

"Oh, I can think of a few things." His hand slid down
to her heat again.

"Will," she gasped. And then she was lost in the
pleasure.

WILL WATCHED HER SLEEP. It was becoming a habit.

He wouldn't have given up this night for anything,
but it had to end. It was only a few hours until his
7:00 a.m. meeting and he had to prepare. This was the
first time his entire attaché team would be assembled.
Sitting on the side of the bed he contemplated what he
should do. It didn't feel right leaving her without some
way of contacting him.

But did he want her to contact him? Hannah's life
was chaotic and crazy, from what he'd experienced of it.
She ran at full throttle all of the time and he had a feeling she didn't think much of schedules. She was exactly
the kind of woman he worked hard to stay away from
and more than ever he needed someone who calmed
him. Maybe even a woman who was a little boring.

The very last thing Hannah was was boring. And
honestly, there wasn't anything wrong with that. But
Will wanted someone to share his life with so they
could grow old together. Not that it would happen anytime soon, as he had at least one more tour to go.

Still, the past few years had taught him that each day
was a gift to be used and appreciated to the full.

Hannah. There was an ethereal quality to her. As if she were a fairy flitting with a magical wand healing his soul. Her magic was strong and he had most definitely fallen under her spell.

And it scared the hell out of him.

4

"SON, I SHOULD HAVE YOU court-martialed." The general slammed down the newspaper with the huge photo of Will's half-naked chest from the runway. "This conduct will not be tolerated. I should have the MPs down here to drag your ass to the brig. Give me one good reason why I shouldn't," he growled.

Will had seen the old man get angry before, but usually it was a quiet steam kind of heat. He never blustered, which meant Will was in big trouble. He'd screwed up royally and he deserved whatever came his way. In his father's mind, a marine as a fashion model was a major infraction. He stared straight ahead and waited for his sentence, knowing the general's previous question was rhetorical.

"Sir," Rafe's voice croaked. Poor guy. It was Will's fault his friend was being raked over the coals.

"I'm not speaking to you, Lieutenant." The general jabbed a finger toward Rafe.

"Yes, sir. But I have information integral to the investigation, sir. Captain Hughes won't admit it, but he didn't have a choice."

The general folded his arms and leaned back on his heels. "Now this I've got to hear." His steely-gray eyes bore into Rafe. Will wanted to kick his friend's butt for interfering. Nothing Rafe could say would help the situation. In fact, it would only make it worse. Of that, Will was certain.

"She cried, sir." Rafe cleared his throat.

"What?" the general asked, exasperated.

"The girl on the street who asked for our help. She said it was a life-and-death situation for her. That she would lose everything if we didn't help her. And she was crying. I mean like sobbing, in the middle of the sidewalk."

The older man seemed to contemplate Rafe's words.

"Is that true, Marine?" The question was aimed at Will.

"Yes, sir."

The general's expression softened slightly. "A damsel in distress, that's what this fiasco is about? If I ask this young woman would she corroborate your story?"

"Sir, yes, sir," Will and Rafe said at the same time.

There was another long silence as the general sat behind his desk.

"I'll need to speak with her."

Will sucked in a breath and his heart sped up like a freight train barreling down a hill with no brakes. Hannah wouldn't last two minutes under the scrutiny of this man. She might have to deal with the women like the Hags, as she called them, but she was no match for the General. No, he couldn't let it happen.

"I'd like to leave the woman out of it." Will's voice came across much stronger than he intended. In the face of danger he'd often been able to keep his nerves dampened down. Marines didn't know fear. But subjecting Hannah to the old man would be nothing less than torture for her. The general was all about rules and regulations. Hannah was creative and followed her whims. He had to protect her. "I'm happy to take my punishment. I deserve it, sir."

"William Washington Hughes, you will have that woman in my office no later than five today. Do I make myself understood? Or you'll face charges for conduct unbecoming an officer." He pointed a finger at Rafe. "It's your duty to make sure he does what I ask. If Sir Galahad here has any notions of protecting his damsel from me, you'd better think twice before going against my order. As for you—" this time he pointed at Will "—if that woman isn't in my office by the deadline your lieutenant is going to the brig. Dismissed."

They both saluted. As Will reached the door the general called out to him. "Marine…"

Will turned. "Yes, sir."

"I meant what I said about your friend and the brig."

Will saluted his father again. Sometimes he really hated the man.

HANNAH WOKE SLOWLY. It was eight-thirty in the morning but she'd slept only four hours. Sitting up on the side of the bed, she stretched. Muscles she didn't even know she owned were sore.

Last night was the kind that spawned legends. Will was a machine. A tender, lovemaking machine. The mere thought of him twisted her insides. She hadn't been surprised that he was gone before she woke up. She'd expected it.

This was his first day on a new assignment and she knew their night had been a singular event. He'd made no promises, nor had she.

You'll probably never see him again. She tried to act as if it didn't matter. They ran in different worlds. It was absurd to think he'd ever return after what she'd put him through the day before.

A knot formed in her gut.

"No. You aren't going to do this. You both blew off some steam last night. You had a great time. Incredible sex and he was everything a man should be. Now let it go."

In the kitchen she poured herself some coffee, the first sip working like a shot of adrenaline to her brain. Everything she needed to accomplish in the next forty-eight hours assailed her.

She was about to reach for her sketchpad when her cell phone rang. She didn't know the number but she picked up anyway.

"Hello?"

"It's Will."

She couldn't stifle the grin that slid across her face. "How did you get my cell? Wait, that sounded like an accusation. I promise I didn't mean it that way. I'm surprised you called."

"I got it off your phone last night and left you my number there on the coffee table."

So maybe last night wasn't the end. She was mad at herself about the excitement that thought sent through her body.

"Oh. So what's up?"

"I have to ask you a favor." He sounded hesitant.

"Will, you saved my beans yesterday. I would do anything for you."

And to you.

"I wouldn't have called you for this if it weren't absolutely necessary." He sounded so serious.

"What's wrong?"

"The general wasn't happy about Rafe and me modeling yesterday. There are pictures all over the paper. We explained that we only did it to help you out, that it was sort of an accident, but he wants to talk to you. If I don't get you to his office before five today, he's going to throw us both in the brig."

"The brig?"

"It's the military's version of a jail."

"No, I know what it is, but it seems extreme. I mean, you weren't wearing your uniforms. I don't understand why he has a problem with it. You were off duty."

Will sighed. "It's tough for civilians to understand, but you are never off duty when you're a marine. We are representatives of the U.S. Marine Corps at all times. If you don't want to do this, I understand." He sounded so dejected.

"Of course I'll do it. I told you I'd do anything for you. Besides, I'd like to give that general a piece of my mind for being so mean to you guys. He should be the one going in the brig."

She thought she heard him laugh. "Might be best if you just go in and tell him the truth about how you met us. He isn't likely to appreciate any kind of confrontation."

"I can do that. I need to shower and find something to wear. I can meet you wherever you need me to in about an hour and a half." She needed most of that time to whip her hair into submission.

5

AN HOUR AND A HALF LATER, dressed in her best Chanel suit trying to look like a proper young woman, she was in a conference room at a hotel near the UN. Will was caught up in meetings so Rafe met her in the lobby and directed her to the room. Earlier Will had explained why she had to be here, and she promised she would do whatever it took to help him.

"The general is…" Rafe looked around the hotel conference room. He pulled out a notepad and wrote *is tough. Room may be bugged.* "Is a nice guy," he said out loud. "Captain Hughes told me to tell you not to worry. If there are questions that make you feel uncomfortable, you don't have to answer. You really don't have to do any of this. The captain and I are more than willing to take our punishment without dragging you into this."

Hannah tore off the piece of paper and stuffed it in her coat pocket. "I'm here to make him understand what really happened," she said. "And I'm not going home until he does."

"That will be all, Lieutenant." A handsome older man walked in through another door Hannah hadn't even noticed.

Rafe saluted. Without saying a word, he backed out of the room.

The man held out his hand and Hannah shook it.

"I'm General Holland Hughes. I appreciate you taking time out of your busy day to assist in this matter."

Intimidating. If there were one word to sum this guy up, that would be it. He was as big as Will, which was saying something, but he had a few more lines on his face and his light brown hair had white at the temples.

Hannah stood a little straighter. She was here to help Will and she'd be damned if she'd let this guy do anything to him or Rafe.

"I'd like for you to share with me your version of what happened yesterday." The general claimed a seat and motioned for her to do the same.

Hannah watched him carefully. Then gave him a sweet smile. "I don't know what you mean by a version of the story. The truth is simple. I was at my wit's end. My entire business was about to go down the drain because my models were missing." She didn't think it would help to mention they were in jail.

"I went out on the street to find someone who might fit the clothes. It was crowded, but I couldn't find anyone who was right for what I needed. Desperate, I started crying. Right there in public. A man comforted me, and told me no matter what was going on, that I would be okay. That man was Captain Hughes."

Hughes? Wait a minute. That was the general's last name, too.

"Are you related to Will?"

"That's irrelevant," he said in a clipped tone.

Hannah wasn't exactly known for putting up with bullies. "Are you this rude all the time or is it some kind of intimidation tactic? You remind me of my dad. Even the way you do your eyebrows. As if you disapprove of everyone, no matter what's going on."

As soon as she finished talking, she wanted to slam a palm to her forehead. The last thing Will and Rafe needed was for her to shoot off her big mouth and make the general angrier.

"Will is my son." His face didn't change, but Hannah had a feeling she'd won some kind of battle.

That bit of information took a second to process. His own father was threatening him with the brig?

He was probably making an example out of his son. Holding him up to even tougher standards than he probably would for anyone else in this situation.

And I'm sure I've made the perfect first impression. This man hates me.

"Thank you for telling me," Hannah said politely as if she hadn't just blown everything by being an idiot. "As I was saying, I begged Captain Hughes and his friend to help me. At the time, I'm not sure I explained fully what it would entail. I just told them I needed big, strong guys and that my life depended on them helping me." She took a breath. "If I had any idea that they would be in trouble for helping a stranger, I would have never asked, even if it had ruined my show. They are amazing men. So kindhearted."

Her mind flashed to the night before when Will's hands covered her body. He sure had been amazing then. The way he teased her into oblivion, her body taut with need—

Stop it!

She hated when her brain did stuff like that at the most inopportune moments. Twice on the subway here she caught herself grinning like the Cheshire cat while thinking about Will.

This is not the time to run your personal porno through your whacked-out head. Pray you didn't have some kind of goofy orgasm face.

Poor Will, he would go to jail and it was all her fault because she couldn't tame her libido.

"They were the hit of the show. With only a few instructions, they performed as if they had been doing it their entire lives. They pushed the show to a new level, and helped to launch my career and my business in a major way. They're like my guardian angels."

That last bit might have been laying it on kind of thick. She decided to stop there. Worried that if she kept talking, she would say something else stupid, she bit the inside of her lip.

"Are you admitting your business would have been in jeopardy if my men hadn't helped you?"

The way he said *admitting* sounded as though he didn't believe her.

Hannah frowned. "Yes. As I said before, the two designs at the end were what really distinguished my line from everything else that is out there. If you aren't distinctive in some way, they forget about you before they leave the show."

The silence sent waves of nausea through her stomach.

Great.

"I understand that perhaps some of the photos might have been upsetting to you." She had to stop talking. "But I promise you those men had the best intentions. When they found out what was required, I could tell they didn't want to go through with it. But they had promised.

"I haven't known either of them for very long, but they are men of their word. What they did was incredibly difficult and perhaps embarrassing for them, but they did it anyway to help out some crazy woman they didn't even know."

There was a knock on the door. "Sir, you have five minutes until the meeting with—" The man seemed to notice Hannah was there. "The meeting, sir."

Must have been some top secret meeting the way the general cut the guy down with his eyes.

But he stood and Hannah did the same. "Again, I appreciate you taking the time to sort this out." He stuck out his hand and she shook it again.

Then he turned to leave.

"Sir." Hannah wasn't sure what to say. "You did a good job with Will. He really is an amazing human being."

The older man nodded and left.

She had no idea if she had helped or hindered the situation, but she'd done her best.

Not sure what she should do next, she left through the door Rafe had brought her in. He was waiting in the hallway.

"Will's really sorry he couldn't be here. I hope the general wasn't too harsh."

Hannah pursed her lips. "It wasn't bad at all, but he's a hard one to read. His face never changed, except when his assistant interrupted the meeting. And it might have been nice if you guys had told me they were related."

Rafe smiled. "He told you that?"

"Only after I asked. He told me it was irrelevant, and I told him that he was rude."

Rafe stopped walking and faced her with a panicked look on his face.

"What?" She acted surprised but she knew why he was upset. She'd really done it this time. Poor guys.

"You talked back?"

"No, not really. I just called him on his attitude. He was trying to be a tough guy with me and I didn't appreciate it."

Rafe sighed.

"I caused more trouble for you and Will, didn't I?"

Rafe pushed the button for the lobby on the elevator panel. "I don't know. He's, well, I don't know. He's pretty hard on Will. I'm just a pawn. You showing up probably cleared me. But Will—"

Her gut churned. "If I did anything else to get him in trouble, I'm never going to forgive myself. I'm sorry to you, too, Rafe."

He put a hand on her shoulder and guided her out to the lobby. "You don't have to worry about me. I was scared as hell last night and I don't scare easy. But I had a great time meeting everyone. And I had one of the best dates of my life thanks to your show."

Hannah's head shot up. "You did?"

"One of the models, Micola. She took me out for Indian food and we talked football until the wee hours of the morning. I never met a woman who looked like that and is better at football stats than I am."

Her hand around her middle, Hannah laughed. "I had no idea she was into sports, either."

"I have no regrets about last night. And like I said before, if the general decides to go hard-core, we can take it. Certainly won't be the first time for Will. He has to live up to a whole different standard than the rest of us."

"I had a feeling that was the case. I'm sorry I didn't get to see him to apologize again. Will you please tell him for me, Rafe?"

"He's cool with it. I promise. He never wanted you to come today. The only reason he called was to keep me out of the brig. We both appreciate you doing this today. No matter what happens. I've got to get going."

Hannah waved goodbye. Outside, snow fell but she didn't care. Even though she was wearing her favorite Marc Jacobs booties. Twice she almost slipped, but she managed to stay upright on the sidewalk.

Never had she been so disappointed in herself. All she had to do was be polite to the general. She had grown up around people like him and she knew what was expected. But she couldn't keep her mouth shut for ten minutes to make that happen.

Then she thought about the past few weeks. How hard she'd been on the staff. No question she'd become a designerzilla the past few days. After years of working for people like that, she'd sworn she would never act that way. Designers as a whole were mercurial at best. One time Leland had screamed at her because he didn't like the color of belt she had chosen to accent one of his designs. She knew she would never act like that. Leland, when he wasn't working, was a dreamboat, but when he was designing or before a show, he was nothing short of evil. And he wasn't the only one.

I thought I was above all that.

Obviously she wasn't. The monster in her had risen to the occasion. She'd used people. Done whatever it took to manipulate them to do what she wanted. She was no better than any other designer she'd ever complained about. In fact, she was even worse. The staff she put together worked with her because she was usually fair and kind. But in the end she'd used them.

Did she have to take advantage of everyone she met? Anne Marie, Jesse, Will and Rafe. They were all being helpful and professional and she—

I'm selfish. The words hurt but they were true. She was used to doing whatever it took to get what she wanted, by whatever means, and she didn't always think about the consequences for the other people involved. That would change.

The very idea that she'd forgotten a promise made her realize how far she'd traveled to the dark side. Years ago she vowed to take care of Anne Marie but she'd been working the poor girl to death. Her friend was always in the studio when she arrived in the morning and when she left at night. There had been some days when it seemed Anne Marie never left. She was so dedicated, and Hannah had thanked her by acting like a complete moron.

What would it be like to put someone's needs first? She wasn't an awful person, but it was time for her to grow up.

Will. He made her want to be a better person. And she was damn sure going to try and prove to him that she could be.

That was, if he ever spoke to her again.

6

"CAPTAIN. A WORD." His father's gruff voice stiffened Will's spine.

For the past hour and a half Will did his best to avoid the man's glare. If anyone deserved to be angry it was Will. His father had made the situation personal when he called in Hannah. Then the old man made it so he couldn't protect her. There hadn't been any meetings scheduled this morning and then suddenly, during the time when Hannah would be downstairs, there was a strategy meeting called. The general was up to his tricks again.

"Yes, sir."

"Follow me." On the elevator ride up to his parents' suite not a word was said. There were others in the elevator and whatever was about to happen, his father wanted privacy.

What did Hannah say?

Earlier the text Rafe sent said:

She's still alive.

He had no idea what that meant. The general could be a real hard-ass when he wanted. He'd be surprised if Hannah ever spoke to him again.

His father had a small suite and he motioned for Will to sit down on the sofa in the living area. His mother was in town, but had probably gone out shopping. She had mentioned to Will that she thought it was exciting that he had been in the fashion show. But she would never tell his father that.

"I talked to the young woman who rooked you into that fiasco."

"Yes, sir."

"She explained the situation. The investigation is over. I would suggest in the future you think about how you are representing the corps before you do something that will embarrass us all.

"And that woman. She obviously has feelings for you. I suggest you break that off as quickly as possible. You don't need that kind of distraction, especially now. There is too much at stake. Your priorities must be your special detail."

"Sir. Are you speaking to me as the general or as my father?" Will's voice was tinged with anger. He couldn't help it. Now the man who had told him what to do all of his life said that he couldn't date Hannah.

"Both, young man. Watch your tone."

"As my father, sir, I can take care of myself. Hannah is a very nice woman and I don't appreciate you telling me who I can see socially."

"I never said she wasn't nice but she is a distraction. One you can ill afford at this point."

He hated that the man was right. He'd been thinking about Hannah all day. Twice during the meeting his superiors had to repeat things because he was worried how his father might be treating her.

There was also the fact Hannah was a woman who deserved the best. He couldn't give her that. She had come from enormous wealth and lived in a different world. Thanks to his investments, he wasn't exactly a pauper but he couldn't afford a loft in New York City. He also didn't have the time to even try to convince her that he was good boyfriend material. Two weeks and he'd be out of here, off to God knew where. "Are we finished, sir?"

His father eyed him carefully. "Yes."

Will stood and saluted.

His mother walked in as he reached the door. He opened it and took the bags from her.

"Hello, sweetie. I'm so happy to see you. Can you stay for lunch?"

After setting the bags on the entry table, Will kissed her cheek. "No, ma'am. I'm sorry. I have another meeting in about twenty minutes." Will gave her a tight smile.

She looked at him and then his father.

"What did you do, Holland?"

"Why do you blame me? He's the one who plastered himself all over the newspapers half-naked."

His mother waved a hand. "Darling, you know I love you, but the only person in the world who cared about those photos was you. My guess is you've been beating this poor boy to the ground because you feel you've been embarrassed in some way. Am I right?"

"I don't have time for this nonsense." The general walked into the bedroom and slammed the door.

"Mom, you shouldn't do that. It isn't worth it."

She wagged a finger at him. "Don't you tell me how to handle your father. I've been married to that man for thirty years. And he loves me because I'm the only who does stand up to him."

Will rubbed his temple with his forefinger and thumb. "Well, don't do it when I'm involved. In the end it backfires on me. I can take it but it isn't worth it. He's trying to tell me who I can and can't date. I don't like him involved in my business. I should have never agreed to this special assignment. I was better off in Iraq."

His mother blanched and her hand went against her chest. "Don't you say that. The two weeks you're here are the only respite I've had in eight years. I worry about you all the time when you're over there. I—" She took a deep breath. "I'm not going to be one of those weepy mothers. But it's hard for me, knowing that every day you put your life in danger."

He wanted to beat his head against the wall for upsetting her. His mother was the one person in the world he could count on. She'd been there for him when no one else had been.

"Sorry, Mom. You know I didn't mean it like that. I just get so tired of him being the general. I'd like to have my dad back some day."

She reached out a hand and patted his shoulder. "I know, honey. And while he will never admit it, he's proud of you—even more so now that you were chosen to be one of the attachés. By the way, he had nothing to do with it. The orders came down from higher up. They're watching you, son, and it has nothing to do with your father."

That surprised Will. He thought for sure his father was meddling in his life again.

"Wait, did you say he was telling you who to date? Does that mean there's a woman in your life? You have to tell me."

Will shook his head. "If I did have a woman, Dad just scared her away by interrogating her, so it's a moot point." That wasn't a lie. "I've got to go now. Love you." He kissed her cheek again.

He was luckier than most. His dad could be a pain but his parents were good people. He wished they'd stay out of his business. Every time he received a promotion or was picked for something like this detail, he wondered if his father had a hand in it. Will worked hard to earn the respect of those around him. When he led his men he was in the trenches with them and never asked them to do anything he wasn't willing to do himself.

He was six blocks away from the hotel standing in the snow before he even realized he'd left.

Distractions.

His father was right. He didn't need any of this at the moment. He had to break it off with Hannah. She deserved someone better—someone who could put up with her fly-by-night lifestyle and be there for her. Will couldn't be that person right now. He wasn't sure if he ever would be. When he did find the right woman, he wanted a stable home and a family. Hannah was embarking on a huge career. They weren't right for each other. It was as simple as that.

Now he needed the courage to call her to do the deed.

7

THE ELEVATOR DOOR TO the penthouse squeaked open and Hannah lifted her head to see Anne Marie carrying two cups of coffee. "Hey, boss? I brought you the good stuff."

"Thanks." Hannah sat cross-legged on her couch working on sketches.

"I didn't want to bug you, but this is— It's really important." The shaking nerves in Anne Marie's voice had Hannah setting down the sketchpad.

"You have my attention."

"I need to ask you a question *but* you have to stay calm when I do." Anne Marie's eyes were guarded. When she set the coffee down on the side table her hand shook. The only time her friend ever showed emotion was when she'd felt she'd done something wrong. Years of living in foster care had given her a complex—she always needed to be perfect in everything she did. And she usually was. The mistake with the male models, which wasn't her fault, was the first time she'd seen her visibly upset.

Anne Marie was the rock and the fixer.

This isn't good.

Hannah's shrugged, trying to keep things calm. "The last time you said something like that I had to borrow two marines off the street to save my show and I almost ruined their lives." The words were harsher than she meant. "I'm sorry. I didn't mean it like that. Tell me."

Her assistant director's jaw tightened and her eyes closed as if she were praying.

"Just spit it out," Hannah blurted. Temper had never been a problem for her but the universe had been slightly wicked to her lately with the super highs and scary lows, and she wasn't sure how much more she could take. She remembered her vow from earlier in the day. She wouldn't be that crazy person ever again.

Don't shoot the messenger.

Remember you aren't that person. You care about Anne Marie and she would do anything to please you.

Hannah reached out and tugged Anne Marie's hand so she had to sit on the sofa with her. "I didn't mean to sound so harsh. I'm running on four hours of sleep over two days and I'm not quite myself. I promise no matter what you say I'll be Zen."

Anne Marie gave her a tight smile as if she didn't believe her. "Do you have the sapphire dress, the sunshine blouse and the denim skirt somewhere up here?" The words rushed out of her mouth so fast, Hannah had to hit the replay button in her head.

"No," Hannah answered, her voice a whisper. It was the only way she could keep from screaming.

The other woman's hands balled into fists and she jumped up dancing from foot to foot. "This is bad. Like end-of-the-world, accidentally-jumped-into-a-black-hole suckage."

Hannah counted to fifteen, as ten simply wasn't enough.

"First—" she forced her voice to be calm "—you need to cut back on those sci-fi and dystopian films you've been watching. Whatever it is, it isn't end-of-the-world bad. Second, take a deep breath. You know how easy it is for clothes to get misplaced on a rack. Or maybe someone accidentally boxed them and they are in the back of the warehouse."

Anne Marie leaned forward. "Hannah," she cried. "Don't you think I checked everywhere before coming up here to bug you? I mean, I'm the organized one. I'm the one who doesn't let things like this happen. I'm the one—"

Hannah held up her hand. "Wait! We'll find them together. You are the organized one and we'll systematically go through everything together. I'm surprised you are even here. I thought maybe you guys were going to take half a day off?"

"There's too much to do before the buyers come in for their appointments. I was in the middle of getting the racks set up when I realized we were missing items. I grabbed the inventory sheet and that's when—" The last word was a sob.

If Anne Marie cried, Hannah wasn't sure she could

hold it together. "You know what? We are both exhausted. I bet you accidentally overlooked something. Let me change and drink some coffee and I'll help you search. Also, call a staff meeting. Let's pull in everyone to help. We'll go through every box in the warehouse if we have to, but you stop worrying. Everything is going to be okay."

Hannah's cell phone rang. When she saw it was Will, she didn't want to answer but her finger clicked the button anyway.

"Hello?" Her voice was shaky. Hannah wondered if it was because of what Anne Marie just told her or the fact that Will was on the other end.

"Hey. I was wondering if I could talk to you." He sounded serious. Great, he was calling to tell her that he couldn't see her anymore. She couldn't blame him. She'd caused him so much trouble. But the timing sucked.

"Hannah?"

"Sorry. I'm in the middle of a crisis right now. Can I call you back later?"

"What kind of crisis?" Will's concern was clear. Why in the hell did he have to be so nice?

"Um, look, I appreciate you acting like you care but you don't have to pretend. You can't see me anymore. I get it, I do. No hard feelings on my part at all. I met your dad. I know how this goes. You're a great guy and I'll be eternally grateful for what you did. I'm really sorry I put your career in jeopardy. But right now I have to deal with this."

There was a slight pause.

"Okay, well have a nice—" She was about to hang up.

"I asked you what kind of crisis." Will's steely reserve didn't give up.

"Will, really—" This would be so much easier if he would just hang up.

"Hannah." There was an edge to his voice.

"We're missing some of the clothes from the show last night and there are buyers who will be coming over tomorrow to sift through designs and put in their orders. Editors will be coming in to see what they might want to feature. My collection isn't that big, so missing pieces are kind of a big deal." Hannah's gut churned. Saying the words out loud made it all seem too real.

"Missing like lost? Or stolen?"

Stolen? Oh, no. She hadn't even thought of that.

"I...have no idea," she said honestly.

"I'll be there in half an hour." The line went dead.

Hannah watched her phone as if it were a tarantula ready to bite.

"So, that was Will?" Hannah had forgotten Anne Marie was standing next to her.

"Yes. He's going to be here in a bit. What time are the buyer appointments?"

"First one was at two today, but I pushed everything to Monday. I told them you were busy with press. You know how they all love clothes with buzz, so it actually worked in your favor."

"Great thinking and one of the many reasons I love

you. Call the shop and warn Kathryn and Brenda that we might need to re-create some of the samples."

"But—" Anne Marie began to interrupt.

Hannah swallowed hard and prayed her voice didn't squeak when she spoke. "I know the beading on sunshine is seventy hours alone. Tell them to start with the skirt. That will only take them a few hours. Hopefully, we'll find everything and then we'll have duplicates. I should have done that in the first place, in case something was ruined during the show."

"No, I should have thought of that." Anne Marie looked grim.

"This is not your fault. My goodness, you were nuts at the show trying to keep up with the models, the press and the guests. I don't know how you do it. I should have double-checked to make sure everything was packed and labeled correctly before we left."

Anne Marie rolled her eyes. "No, you are the designer. You sketch and create. I take care of the business. This is on me and don't even try to say it isn't. You tell me all the time I'm a machine and that's what makes me special. I just flat-out screwed up and it isn't the first time in the last twenty-four hours." Her friend's voice was hoarse.

"Oh, don't be upset because you know I won't be far behind. You are my amazing machine. That photographic memory of yours is going to help us get back on track and we are going to figure this out. Now go. Do your thing and rally the troops."

Anne Marie gave a small salute and turned to leave.

"Uh...?" Hannah wasn't sure how to say it.

"Yes." The other woman turned back to Hannah.

"Will is going to be here so let's not do any more saluting. I don't want to risk accidentally insulting him. They're kind of particular about that sort of thing."

"Got it!" Anne Marie curtsied.

If her life wasn't in such a terrible mess, Hannah might have smiled.

"YOU'RE AN IDIOT," whispered Will as he thumped his head lightly against the bathroom door. What was he thinking? She'd given him an out. Told him that she understood and it caused his stomach to sink with despair. The idea of never seeing her again wasn't an option. So he'd volunteered to help her.

Yes, it isn't like you have world leaders to protect or anything.

What had his father said about distractions?

He shoved his shirt into his jeans and opened the door. Rafe was at the desk typing on the computer. They'd finished the revised plans and now Rafe was making sure everyone knew where they had to be at the appointed time.

"Why were you beating up the door?"

"I have to help Hannah."

Rafe stood. "But the general said——" He cut himself off. "Did she call you?"

"No. I was setting up a meeting with her so I could break it off and, well, there's nothing really to break off. We just met. In fact, I think she was trying to give me any easy out. But she was upset about some of her clothing that has possibly been stolen."

"You know I'm in. When do we go?"

"There is no *we*. You aren't getting in any deeper. One of us needs to stay out of trouble. If the general gets wind of this, I'm not bringing both of us down."

"What's to find out? We're going to her shop, I would assume, to talk with her. There's no harm in that. Besides, we work well as a team."

Rafe had a point. Plus it would be easier to keep Hannah at arm's length with his friend there. His first instinct on hearing the panic in her voice had been to reach through the phone and fold his arms around her. Yes, having Rafe as a buffer wouldn't be such a bad thing. His friend was excellent at staying on task, especially in the middle of a crisis.

When Will had been shot the first time, it was Rafe who helped him keep the men organized. He only had to whisper orders and Rafe made sure everything was done. His friend's quick thinking had helped them out of a tight situation. And the pressure he kept on Will's shoulder where the bullet had punctured an artery probably saved his life.

"Sir?"

His head shot up. "It's your funeral, Marine. We do this and it's on the covert. Got it?"

Rafe smiled as he loaded his laptop in the backpack he carried everywhere. "Sir, yes, sir."

Will grimaced. "Cut the crap. These are artsy types and I don't want you making them nervous. They have to be coddled. When we're around her people you're my friend, Rafe."

"Yep, but I like giving you a hard time."

"That you do."

Two subway rides later they were in front of her shop. He tried not to think about the way she kissed him. Or the way she smelled of exotic flowers. The look in her eyes when she—

"Sir?"

"Stop calling me that when we're alone."

"Habit. I think you have to push the buzzer. Unless one of them is psychic."

Will gave him a withering look and tried not to notice Rafe's grin.

He pushed the buzzer and though they didn't hear anything, the door clicked open. They stepped into a darkened hallway as Hannah came around and switched on the light.

"That's not very good security letting anyone who buzzes in." Will's words sounded accusatory. He'd spoken as if he was talking to one of his men.

Her eyes narrowed and she pointed behind him. "Security cameras."

She turned on her heel and didn't give him another glance.

"Smooth," he heard Rafe whisper.

Why did he ever think it would be a good idea to bring his friend along? Hannah was angry with him now. Why couldn't he have at least said hello?

Rafe cleared his throat, which propelled Will into action as he followed Hannah through the hallway.

8

HANNAH HAD TO ADMIT it was a rocky start with Will that evening but his and Rafe's mad detective skills genuinely impressed her. At first he'd been grumpy but then they'd both jumped in and organized everyone into groups. In less than an hour they'd talked to all of her employees about the show. Rafe had even called all the models they used to see if they had seen anything. Through the staff's accounts, the marines discovered there was a five-minute window when the clothes might have been taken.

Lincoln Center—where her show had been—was a high-traffic area, especially during Fashion Week, and there were cameras staged at almost every street corner and on most of the buildings. Rafe was on the phone with his friend Tag, who worked with the NYPD. Once they had determined when the designs were taken, Will had insisted they bring in the police to make if official.

"Tag says they've narrowed it down to two video clips," Rafe said. His cell phone was in the crook between his ear and shoulder as he pulled out his laptop. "Some of the other cameras were either too far away or were angled wrong. He's sending them over."

Hannah took a deep, cleansing breath.

"Don't get your hopes up," Will said from behind her. "The cameras have to be at just the right angle for us to pick up anything."

"Are you always this negative?" The words left her lips before she could stop them.

He didn't flinch but his eyes blinked quickly as if she'd slapped him.

The studio, which was swarming with "her people," as Will called them, was silent.

Jeez, Hannah. He's helping you and this is the way you thank him.

"There's no excuse for that," she said quickly. "I'm really tired and worried. Again. No excuse."

Will winked at her. "It's okay. I'm a marine. I can take it."

For the first time in several hours she smiled. Everyone on the other side of the room laughed and started talking again. Anne Marie, Jesse and Kayleigh were there, along with some of the other interns and warehouse staff.

"For the record, I'm pragmatic," Will said. "I saw how excited you were and I wanted you to be prepared."

Reaching out a hand she touched his forearm. The big muscle twitched but he didn't pull away. If she were a weaker woman she would throw herself into those arms and bury her face in his oh-so-solid chest.

He took the hand on his arm and held it as they moved behind Rafe.

"At least it is something," she said. "Even if we can't see, it's validation that something happened and that we just didn't misplace the clothes somewhere."

"True," Will said.

"No matter what we do or don't see, I am grateful to both of you for all you've done. You knew exactly how to pinpoint the problem. You're so smart about this stuff."

Will squeezed her hand.

"Hannah, you hit the mother lode when it comes to Captain Hughes," Rafe said. "He's the best when it comes to security and that's why the bigwigs—"

"Marine!" Will's voice sounded a warning.

"I thought you were going to call me Rafe around the artsy people. Besides, she should know she has the best," Rafe said without looking up. "Here we go." His fingers flew across the keyboard.

His laptop screen was seventeen inches, but it was still difficult to see anything. At first the images were so dark she couldn't make out shapes.

"That's the van." Hannah pointed to the left of the screen. The white vehicle was the only thing that popped out of the blackness.

Rafe blew up the image and moved the video forward frame by frame. The next shot showed Anne Marie and Jesse loading the van. They both left and then there was a figure in black wearing a hat. The person walked up to the van, looked to the left and the right, took clothes off the rack and ran.

Hannah's heart was in her throat. "Who is that?" she managed to ask.

"You have to tell us," Rafe said.

Will leaned down and pushed a few buttons. "It's either a woman or small man. Very slim. The back is always to the camera. It's almost as if the thief... Hannah, this was premeditated. This person knew exactly what they were going for and when to hit you at the right time."

She growled in frustration. "Please tell me there's a better photo of the face because I really want to see who I need to kill."

She thought she heard Will chuckle. When she gave him an evil glance he was staring straight ahead with no hint of humor on his face.

Rafe enhanced the photo again but it became nothing but a blurry haze. "I thought we might catch a reflection but there's no light out there. It's pitch-black. They should have put security lights around there for you guys," Rafe pointed out.

Will turned to look at Hannah. "Why aren't the interior lights working?"

"I— They burned out a few months ago and I didn't know how to replace the fuse."

He nodded. "Does the shape of the person look like anyone you might know? Maybe the way they move?"

Rafe rewound the video and played it over and over.

"No." She sighed. "It could be half the people in New York City."

Will glanced back at the others, who had gathered around, but they all shook their heads.

"No distinguishing marks. With the clothing, and the way the person held their back to the camera, Captain Hughes is right. This was planned." Rafe copied the digital file. "I'm going to send this to you guys. Maybe you can put it on a bigger screen in better light."

"Is there anyone you know who would want to hurt your business? Someone with professional jealousy?" Will turned her to face him.

"In the fashion world it could be anyone," chimed in Anne Marie. "There's a lot of money to be made if those designs go to mass market."

Will frowned. "But there is photographic and witnessed evidence that these designs are hers," he said without turning away from Hannah. She wished she didn't like how much he seemed to care about what was going on. This was no act. He was concerned for her.

"Yes," Hannah said, "but they change something on a pocket, send it overseas and a week later, it's in every discount store in the country. That's why we are so protective of what we do."

The enormity of what had happened hit her all at once and tears burned. She tried to pull away, but Will held her in his arms and squeezed her tight. It was her undoing. She wept silently into his shirt.

"We should go restack the boxes we went through out in the warehouse. Those things aren't going to sort themselves out." Anne Marie shooed everyone out.

"Rafe, why don't you go see if you can help?" Will suggested.

A chair scraped against the floor.

"Well, this isn't embarrassing or anything." She

sniffed and he handed her a tissue from the table. They'd put out a box because a cold front had come through giving everyone the sniffles. The frigid temperatures had done nothing for her mood. Hannah preferred warm sunshine and beaches to slippery sidewalks and dirty snow. "Thanks. I'm not usually one of those girls who cries all the time."

Will shrugged. "You have every right to be upset. If it were me I'd probably be beating the hell out of a punching bag."

She smiled at that. "I'm not usually big on violence, but I could seriously put the hurt on whoever did this. It isn't just about me. They've taken money away from all those people in that warehouse. Everyone of them has a stake in Hannah Harrington designs. They all worked so hard. It isn't fair and I want to make the jerk who did this pay. I can always come up with more designs and we can even re-create the designs for the buyers. But if they're in discount stores in forty-eight hours or anytime soon, then they aren't going to be as special."

He gave her another squeeze.

"Well, then, we need to find out who did this before that can happen. Rafe was right. I am pretty good at this sort of thing."

Hannah touched his cheek. "You're so sweet. But honestly, it's most likely too late. The designs are probably halfway to China or Taiwan by now. And the job you have to do here is so much more important." She didn't know exactly what it was but he was security and he was working on a special assignment with the United Nations, so it was probably saving the world big-time.

"What you do is important, Hannah."

She laughed. "Man, you've come a long way in the last twenty-four hours."

"I had a good teacher." His phone rang, and when he glanced at the number he grimaced. "I have to take this."

He backed away and Hannah automatically missed his strong arms.

You can't think that way. Remember, he was about to tell you that he could never see you again. Before you dragged him into your drama.

"Yes. Got it." He ended the call and stuffed his phone in his pocket. "I'm sorry. Rafe and I have to go immediately. But I promise we'll follow up with you. The police may contact you to see if you have any more information. Hannah, it all seems kind of impossible, but believe me, it's going to work out."

The way he looked at her, she wasn't sure if he was talking about the clothes or their relationship. Before she could ask, Rafe walked in and stuffed his laptop in his backpack. "Sir, he said twenty-three-hundred hours, that doesn't give us much time." Obviously, Rafe had received the same call as Will.

"You guys go save the world. Don't worry about this. We'll figure it out."

"Tag and his guys are on this and we will work it from our end, too," Rafe promised. "I hate people who steal, and trust me, we'll make them pay."

"Rafe, thank you. Both of you…" She looked up at Will. "It's— Just thanks."

"No problem," Will said. He started to walk away

and stopped. He turned back and kissed Hannah. She'd been so surprised that her mouth had been in a slight O when he captured her lips and he teased her with this tongue. When he pulled back, she took a deep, shuddering breath.

The man's kisses were nothing short of dangerous. Straight to the soul, wrap-up-your-heart-and-tie-it-in-a-bow scary.

If she wanted to see him again, she had to keep things simple.

"Thanks, Marine, for coming out on yet another damsel-in-distress call."

"Not a problem, ma'am. It's what we do." Will smiled.

He gave her another quick peck on the cheek and left with Rafe.

Hannah could do little more than wave.

"I think he might be into you." Jesse's comment made her jump.

The tattooed fabric genius grinned.

"So what happens next?" Anne Marie returned to the studio.

Hannah shook her head. "Maybe the police will turn up something, but it's not like we have the skills to become the next Scooby Gang. Since we have no idea who did this, we start over. It sucks, but that's life."

Anne Marie ducked her head.

"Hey." Hannah reached out to her but she ran past and out the door. "Wait—" But it was useless. Her friend was gone.

"How many times do I have to tell her I don't blame

her? She better not cry over this crap." Anne Marie was so tough. Probably she just needed a moment to compose herself.

"You cried," Jesse reminded her. "Are you saying she doesn't have the same right to be upset?"

"Stop using logic, Jesse. You know how much I hate it."

He harrumphed. "She feels guilty. Hell, we both do. We were right there, not thirty feet away. Whoever did this had balls."

"I wouldn't have locked the van, either," Hannah said. "We never do. It's friggin' Fashion Week and there are people everywhere. She needs to get over it."

"Hannah, that's not fair." Jesse crossed his arms. "She doesn't show it, but you know how sensitive she is and she's the one who keeps this place running. When you're off searching for the perfect inspiration and networking, she's the one making sure the bills get paid. She lives and breathes this place as much as you do."

A sharp retort was on her tongue but she held it. He was right. How many times had she run off to India or China and left her friend to handle everything? When she missed appointments because she was on a creative binge, it was Anne Marie who always smoothed everything over.

"Jesse, I'm aware of how hard she works." She couldn't keep the edge from her voice.

"It isn't just her. The people who work for you are so loyal. They would do anything for you. Hell, you've sucked me in and I'm not one who does that sort of thing. So it didn't just happen to you. It's more than a job, and someone screwed us all royally with this."

"For an intern, you have a big mouth."

He laughed. "That's a problem I've had all my life."

"If you were wrong, your ass would be so fired right now." She squeezed the bridge of her nose with her thumb and forefinger. "I'm tired. Tell the gang to take half the day off tomorrow. We won't have any appointments until late afternoon. We could all use a break." She took a step. "Please," she added.

"Yes, ma'am, boss."

Hannah's shoulders folded in as she stomped upstairs.

"This day really sucks."

9

LOADED WITH COFFEE and gluten-free beignets from Mozos, Hannah headed into Anne Marie's office. It wasn't much more than a cubby, but her friend liked small spaces. Hannah had offered to give her one of the lofts that had been divided on one of the upper floors, but Anne Marie wouldn't take it.

She'd grown up in foster homes all over Brooklyn. Anne Marie shared stories about some of the homes and swore that she was luckier than most kids in the system. But she had always shared a room with someone. She was used to tight quarters.

The night after she heard some of the stories about her friend never having a space of her own, Hannah had cleaned out the storage closet they used for fabrics and made Anne Marie an office. At that time the studio was much smaller, before they knocked out the walls to make it bigger last year.

When Anne Marie walked in and saw the office, she'd fallen to her knees and held her head in her hands.

She didn't cry exactly, but she made big gulping sounds as if she were trying to catch her breath. At first Hannah was afraid she'd offended her in some way, but Anne Marie promised she'd just been overcome. It was the first time Hannah realized that she needed to make her business a success so that she could take care of her friend.

For the second time, recently, she chided herself forgetting the vow she'd taken that day. Anne Marie had always been so eager to take on responsibility, and Hannah, who hated the business side of things, was more than willing to let her do so. But not anymore. It was time for her to grow up and become a more active leader in this empire she was creating.

"Hey, *chica,* I come bearing coffee goodness and sugary apologies." Hannah turned the corner to find Anne Marie hunkered down at her desk. Then she noticed the other woman was on the phone.

"It's no problem at all. We'll be ready. She'll have more pieces to add to the show. Forty-five minutes is great. Yes, this is a hard confirmation. Please tell him we appreciate the opportunity."

She hung up the phone but kept her head down.

"Anne Marie? What's wrong? Whatever it is, we'll be okay. I promise." That last bit had come out hoarse.

Anne Marie raised her head and the little pixie was beaming.

"When you go off to those ashrams in Los Angeles and India, you always come back spouting about how we need to open ourselves to the universe. That if we have good intentions, good things will happen."

Hannah had no idea where this was going, but she was grateful for the smile on her friend's face. She placed the coffee and pastries on Anne Marie's desk. "Yes."

"Well, last night I was on the floor of my apartment bawling my eyes out." She glanced away. "I know, I know. I never cry. I can't even remember ever crying before. But I'd had enough. The world was too over-whelming and I wanted to crawl into a fetal position and die."

"Oh—" Hannah only said one word before her friend held out a hand.

"My breakdown lasted exactly twenty minutes. Jesse came over and told me that I needed to get over it. He can be so mean sometimes, but he was right."

Hannah smirked. He hadn't liked it so much when she'd said basically the same thing. Hypocrite. "Wait, Jesse came over? Since when do you two hang out to-gether? I thought you fought all the time."

"We don't always see eye to eye on things. But he's my friend and he was worried about me. And so not the point. Stay focused. Anyway, I asked the universe for some good news. When I came in this morning I had a bazillion emails. Most of them are press contacts or editors who want to talk to you. Some were buyers who want to stop by tomorrow. Though, I don't think we have any appointments open. We'll have to ask Kay-leigh. I assigned that to her."

Hannah didn't want to be rude, but if Anne Marie didn't get to the point soon, she might have to throttle her. "And you fussed at me for staying on task."

"Okay. Soooo, I get here this morning and there was an email from Eve Slendean from Fashion House Select in London. They're partnering with John McIntire at Marqu Vodka for their Fashion Week and they're sponsoring hot, young talent. Well, you're hot and young and they want you. John saw your show and told Eve that he wanted you there. They're actually making room for you. You're booked on the main night at the Shade House."

The information had come so fast that Hannah couldn't process it. "Wait, you mean we're showing in London?"

"Uh, yeah. And you're going to be paired with Claron Couture. They're like Chanel of the London set."

Hannah fell onto the small stool in front of her friend's desk. "London?"

Anne Marie laughed. Then something passed over her face.

"What?" Hannah still couldn't complete a sentence. This was beyond anything she could have imagined. First New York, now London. It was too much.

"It's in two weeks and you have forty-five minutes."

Hannah's hand flew to her mouth and she shook her head. "We only have a twenty-five-minute show. Didn't you tell them?"

"Well, the thing is, they told me that we had to do it this way. We have to come up with some new designs for the show because they want everything to be fresh. I mean, you can show what you had here, but they expect for you to add to it."

Hannah's mind whirled. More? Now? She was so

burned out from getting ready for the show the other day she didn't know if she could do it. What if she couldn't come up with something in time? They had to get the designs made and her seamstresses were already working double-time to replace the designs that were taken.

"Stop it!" Anne Marie's sharp demand broke into Hannah's downward spiral.

She focused on her friend's face.

"What?"

"You're doing that thing where you spin out of control and it takes me days to get you out of the funk. This is great news. An opportunity of a lifetime. Pull yourself together. Walk over to that drafting table and draw designs until your fingers fall off."

Hannah's eye twitched.

"Please, don't even think of yelling at me. You forget I grew up on the mean streets of Brooklyn," Anne Marie added. "You were talking about the simple coat you wanted to do. And there was a men's jean design that we didn't have time to do this last time." From the corner of her desk she picked up one of Hannah's design journals. "You left this here last week and I keep forgetting to give it to you. My guess is that flirty skirt with the petal shapes would also be a good one."

"You looked in my journal?"

Anne Marie shrugged. "You left it on my desk for a week. I might have picked it up. Are you off the ledge?"

Hannah nodded. Her friend was right. She could do this. She already had several ideas she'd been playing with and they could easily be mocked up for the show.

She would ask Kathryn and Brenda to hire more help. There was no way they could do this on their own.

"I'll need—"

"I've already called in Jesse. He stopped by the fabric store and picked up some of that denim you like. And he told me to tell you that he found something new that is going to make you do your happy dance."

Hannah laughed. She couldn't help it. "After yesterday, I'm surprised you guys even showed up for work today. In fact, I'm pretty sure I told Jesse that everyone should take half a day off. And you—you were so upset and—"

"I was a basket case yesterday because I was exhausted. You aren't the only one who hasn't slept in weeks. I got a good eight hours in last night and I'm a new woman. No more tears. Now quit lollygagging and get to work."

"Lollygagging?"

Anne Marie joked, "Something one of my foster moms would say when we weren't doing our chores the way she wanted. I think she was from the South."

Picking up one of the cups of coffee, Anne Marie handed it to Hannah along with the journal. "Go!" she ordered.

Anne Marie was back to her old self, and Hannah couldn't be happier. Oh, she was scared to death about London, but her friend was right. She could do this. Hannah sat down at the table in front of the large expanse of windows looking out on to the Hudson. This was one of her favorite spots. Many times she'd thought about moving her table upstairs but she enjoyed being down in the design studio with everyone else.

Placing paper on the surface, she pulled her colored pencils down where she could reach them. Her fingers moved across the sheet before her mind even engaged. Everything from the NYC show to the night with Will flooded her mind, random thoughts ping-ponging around her brain.

The way he touched her, and that look in his eyes when he'd brought her to orgasm. His abs slightly hidden behind the shirt she'd designed. The way he'd protected her at the party from the "ugly hearts," as she liked to call them.

"Are you doing portraits now?"

She jumped.

"Jesse. When did you get here?"

"About twenty minutes ago. You've been in your own little world. I've been talking to Anne Marie about London. Very cool for you."

"Very cool for us. What did you mean about portraits?"

He motioned toward her paper.

Hannah glanced down and realized she'd drawn a pretty good likeness of Will in a suit. She'd never done that kind of detail on men's clothing, but this could be a first. "Uh, inspiration."

"Whatever you say, boss."

She twisted around on her stool to face him. "Bossy over there mentioned you had something to show me."

"Close your eyes," Jesse teased. "No, really, I want you to feel it before you see it."

Hannah did what he asked and held out her hands. It was as if he'd spilled liquid onto her palms, except that it had texture. Opening her eyes she saw the aquamarine jewel-toned fabric was like the ocean in her hands. "It's glorious. I mean like kneel-down-and-praise-God-for-all-the-wonders-of-the-world glorious. Where did you find it?"

"My friend Gringy is an artist who works in different mediums. He's trying different dyes on silk. He has three bolts of this stuff and I bought it all."

"I love how brilliant you are, Jesse. Is there any chance he can make more if we need it?"

He shrugged. "Gringy is meticulous about writing down every step of his process, but you know how it is when you're working with dyes. It may not be quite the same the next time, but it would be close enough."

"This is— It would be perfect for the dress." She opened the journal and flipped the pages until she found the drawing. "See what I mean."

He pointed to the neckline. "What if we did a slight V-neck so that the fabric could drape on the décolleté?"

Hannah erased the scoop neck she had, and drew what he suggested. "I like it. How fast do you think it will take you to mock it up?"

"Couple of hours at the most. I'll get on it. What about your sketch there? I like the shirt."

She studied the paper for a moment. "Yes. Except it's fall, so let's make it a shorter sleeve. And I want to do it Western style with the snaps like the others. But I want this kind of stitching on the collar and cuffs." She showed him what she'd done on the design.

"That reminds me. I have something else to show you," he said.

Jesse swapped the fabric he'd given her for a cotton one. "This is something new Coco got in at the store."

"It's so soft. The deep plum would be perfect for fall. What do you think of the shirt in this?"

"That's what I was thinking. Do you want the stitching in a lighter thread, say a tan? Or black?"

"Hmm. Can you mock it up both ways?"

"Sure. Robbie and Stacks are coming in to help Kathryn and Brenda with the remakes and now they can stitch these, too."

"Excellent."

"Well, you better get back to that before Anne Marie has a fit." They both looked up to find her friend watching them with her arms crossed and a not-so-happy look on her face.

"You might be right about that."

Hannah turned back to her table and pulled out a new sheet of paper. For the past three months she'd lost her passion for what she was doing. Oh, she still loved designing but everything had been so difficult and rushed. They were still rushed, but the fabrics had given her inspiration. Focusing on the best way to use them would be tough.

It isn't just the fabrics.

No, she had to admit Will was a big part of her sudden creative binge.

He'd been going to tell her why he couldn't see her again. His tone when she'd answered the phone had said it all. The fact that even though he'd been about to do it and came to help her anyway, only confirmed what a great man he was.

Will was her new muse. Her mind was so full of ideas she couldn't stop sketching and it was because of him. That inner strength and quiet demeanor spoke of determination and mystery. Her new spring line could be a throwback to the mysteries from the classical age of Hollywood. Even better the inspiration could be early 1940s films. She had always wanted to do a Katharine Hepburn–type wide-legged trouser.

Stop. Focus. Write all this down and then get back to business. None of that will fit in your line for spring, which is what you have to work on now.

After spending a few moments writing down her ideas, she picked up her phone.

Hannah wasn't exactly without feminine wiles. The captain had serious doubts about dating her, and she understood why. But she needed her muse. He was a pragmatic man. He'd said so himself.

Hannah was about to make him a deal he couldn't refuse.

10

WILL SAW HANNAH through the window of the coffee shop she'd suggested. The sight of her honey-colored hair was enough to send his body to attention. The graceful, tapered fingers wrapped around the mug reminded him of their night together and how her hands teased and taunted his body.

The woman is dangerously beautiful.

Her call surprised him. Though he was reluctant to do so, he had to make her understand that he couldn't see her anymore. Rafe was on top of the investigation about the stolen designs. In fact, he had news to report on that front. But he planned to tell her that his schedule was insane for the next week and a half. It wasn't a lie. The summit would begin in a few days, and everything had to be meticulously planned out.

No one felt the powerful connection between them more than he did, but it wasn't fair to lead her on. He tried to think of it as letting her go. She was like a butterfly that deserved to live free and easy. His world, hell, his soul, was dark and dank. There would always be a part of him that he would have to hide from her. Will honestly worried that some of his darkness would rub off on her, cool her optimism. He would never forgive himself for that.

No. He had to do this.

He opened the door and stepped into the warmth of the shop. Hannah smiled at him, and it was as if the sun had exploded in his chest. Never in his life had he reacted to a woman like this.

You're doing this for her own good.

Her hand was drawing on her sketchpad even as she looked up.

It seemed strange not to kiss her cheek after they had been intimate, so he did, inhaling vanilla and honeysuckle, knowing those smells would be forever tied to this woman.

She touched his jaw and he had to sit down quickly to hide the evidence of what she'd done to him.

What are you, fourteen? Get a grip, man.

"Hey," she said and reached across the table to cover his hand with hers.

It was wrong, but he couldn't resist wrapping her fingers in his.

"I see you're working." Will wasn't sure what to say. He did know he had to ease into the conversation. She wasn't one of his men. It was his job to make her understand why he was such a bad choice for her.

She put the pencil down. "Yes. I've had a sudden rush of inspiration. I can't seem to stop."

"Well, I won't keep you long."

"Will, I'm the one who called you, remember?" She tapped her forehead with a finger as if to remind him. "I have to talk to you about something important, but first I wanted to ask you about the investigation. You said you had news."

"Rafe talked to Tag. You weren't the only designer hit during Fashion Week. There were over thirty designs stolen in all. Most of the designers hadn't even realized it until Tag began questioning them. I had no idea how big this fraud business was. They have an entire task force dedicated to it and they're going through the security tapes from the times during the robberies. Hopefully, something will turn up soon."

Hannah squeezed his hand. "You mean, we actually helped out other designers by reporting the theft? I'm glad you made us do it. I hadn't wanted to deal with the police, since I figured it was too late anyway. But this is much bigger than just me. Thank you."

Will shifted in his seat. "I wanted to help you." He had to focus on his objective.

"Yes, but you didn't have to do it. You had called that evening to break it off with me, but you helped instead. That says a lot about you."

How could she know?

"Oh, don't look so surprised. I'm not an idiot. And honestly, I don't blame you a bit. The last thing you need right now is a chaotic chick like me. Your father nearly blew a gasket over those photos and I don't blame him or you. I put your career in danger."

"Hannah, it wasn't that bad. My dad was doing his best to make a point. And I'm beginning to wonder if he wasn't more curious about the kind of woman who could make me get up on stage as a male model. I'm sort of known for following the rules."

She smiled. "I like that about you. You're so solid and strong, physically and mentally."

Will didn't know about the mental part. He held it together, but some days were better than others. His past two tours had really beaten him down.

"There's something I need to tell you." Hannah's voice invaded his thoughts. "And I promise there won't be any hard feelings if you say no."

He was curious.

"Okay."

"I'm a damsel in distress and I need you, more than ever. My future depends on you saying yes, but no pressure, or anything."

Will leaned back in his chair and eyed her warily. *Now what?*

HANNAH ENJOYED the surprise on Will's face. Oh, she was a horrible person for using the damsel-in-distress card. She knew all about his sense of duty and she was evil for playing on it. But she hadn't lied. This was important.

"I'm listening," he said.

"You believe that I'm a huge distraction and perhaps I am. You're a big distraction for me, too, but in a good way. And I think I might be able to help you out the same way."

"I'm not often confused, but you aren't making any sense."

She scrunched her face. This wasn't going quite the way she wanted.

Stop with the manipulation and just tell him the truth. He's a guy who values that.

"As strange as it may sound, you are now my muse. I don't know how or when it happened, and trust me when I tell you I certainly didn't plan it this way. You're the inspiration behind some new design ideas I have for my fall collection, and my idea for my spring collection is absolutely because of you."

"Hannah, I'm not going to model. I'm sorry."

She laughed so hard she had trouble catching her breath.

"Oh, Will, I would never do that to you again. I promise."

"So what is it you want?" His words were cautious and she had to be careful about how she proceeded.

"Let me explain the benefits to you first, and then I'll explain my side."

He nodded.

"So, like I said before about pulling your focus. You were doing the same for me, but then it turned into something else."

Ugh. She still wasn't getting it right.

"Will, I want you to be honest with yourself and me. If you walked out of this coffee shop tonight and never spoke to me again, would I be less of a distraction? Could you put me on some shelf in that brain of yours and pack me away? No more Hannah?"

Her stomach churned at those words.

What if he says yes?

Will glanced up at the ceiling as if he were thinking hard about it.

"No," he said with a sigh.

Hannah bit back a smile. Poor guy, but she could so relate. "I feel the same way about you. I could do the right thing and let you go tonight, but it's not going to stop me from thinking about you."

He leaned forward. "You may be right. You're in my every waking thought. If I couldn't see you, I'd be wondering all the time about what you were doing and if you were okay."

"That's the way I feel. I haven't known you long, but— This is going to scare the hell out of you, but never seeing you again would cause a hole in my heart the size of the Grand Canyon."

Will seemed to contemplate this. "What did you mean about your business?"

"I'm getting to that. So, you're all uptight and stressed about saving the world."

"Hannah, I'm not saving the world. I'm just an attaché. I'm protecting people. No different than a bodyguard, really."

She scoffed. "Bodyguard my ass. You're protecting world leaders and don't make light of it. That's beside the point. When you're at work, it's really intense. But in the few moments you can get away to hang out with me, you can blow off steam. Have some fun."

He frowned.

"We both know this is short-term. I leave for London in a week and you'll be leaving for wherever. So we have a few days to spend with each other and have a good time. That is, when we're not working. Let's make the most of it."

"You're the kind of woman who wants flowers and romance. You deserve it," he said. "I'm not that guy. I see those things as frivolous and silly. I'm more practical—well, usually. That night with you was an aberration. I never— When I'm working that is where my focus has to be."

Hannah grunted. She'd expected this. That night they first met he'd let his guard down and now he was trying to back up a few paces. She understood. She felt the same way. What they'd shared that night had been intense and it had caught them both off guard.

"But we've already established that even if we didn't see one another we would still have trouble focusing. If we have a set time when we know we can be together and we know that's coming, then we can be more committed to the work. And I can buy myself flowers, thanks. I do it weekly. And trust me when I tell you that you are fantasy enough for a hundred women.

"I'm not expecting anything from you, Will. I'm the one person in the world who doesn't want anything, except to be in your presence. You've become inspirational for me. Yes, I have to be truthful about that. But all I'm asking is just to go on a few dates and maybe, if you're up for it, some more great sex." She winked at him.

"That sounds like a challenge."

"Whatever works."

He laughed. "You don't play fair, Hannah. Anyone ever tell you that?"

"What's that saying, all is fair in love and war? You should know that better than anyone."

"Yes, but it would still feel like I was leading you on. I can't make promises about the future. I have no idea what the hell my future is."

Hannah sighed. "Stop being such a man. No one knows what the future holds. Please understand me. I'm not asking you for anything. And I'm sorry, but you don't know what I want. My career is finally taking off. The last thing I need is a relationship. Why can't we just have fun for a week and a half or so and then go our separate ways?" She crossed her arms.

Something passed over his face but it was gone before she could get a read on it.

"You say that, but you don't mean it."

"I'm sick of people telling me what I do and don't mean. Am I attracted to you? Yes. Are you attracted to me? You can deny it all you want, but I know you are. That's enough for me right now. In fact I'm pretty much up to here—" she pointed to the top of her head "—with commitments. I'm turning my life around. Trying to be a responsible human being. There are a lot of people counting on me. So a fling is about all I can handle right now."

He grunted. "So I'm some kind of stress relief."

A smile spread across her face. "Like a good ole trip to the gym. And I'm the same for you. No strings. No commitments. We make love. We hang out. We have a good time. When the time is up, I'm off to London and you go…wherever it is you have to go."

There was a long pause as they both thought about what she'd promised.

Will stuck out his hand. "Deal."

She shook it. "Jeez. Now can we commence with the having fun?"

Her phone buzzed. And her calendar lit up.

"Oh, hell. I forgot about the stupid show."

"What show?"

"I have a front-row seat at the Zac Langfrad event in about an hour. I have to go. He's one of the designers who has been so supportive of me from the beginning. And it's a huge deal to get to sit on the front row of his show. People kill for those seats. Um, I have a plus-one. I don't suppose you'd be my date?"

No way in hell would he say yes.

"You're asking me to go to a fashion show."

She cocked her head and gave him her sweetest smile. "Yes." She had a sudden inspiration. "And if you do, I promise you a surprise you'll never forget."

Will smiled. "Oh, really."

She laughed. "Not sex. Well, that might be how the night ends. But something really cool before that."

"I say we go let off steam, and skip the rest," Will suggested.

Hannah giggled. She was glad to see his sense of humor had returned. "Gutter brain. Trust me, you won't want to miss this surprise."

Will sighed. "Well, how can I say no?"

Hannah leaned across the table and kissed him hard.

"And I promise you all the stress relief you want later tonight," she said against his lips.

"Deal," he said before capturing her lips again.

11

11

WILL SURVEYED THE backstage area of the fashion show. The marine part of him couldn't resist the urge to look for suspicious behavior. He kept a close eye on the clothing, while Hannah visited with her friends.

Never would he admit it to her, but he hadn't minded the Zac Langfrad show. Watching beautiful women walk down a runway wasn't such a hardship, though, Will was tempted to buy them all a bag of hamburgers to share. They were too thin for his taste. He much preferred Hannah's curves.

They had gone behind the stage so Hannah could hug her designer friend, then she had promised him a surprise.

He couldn't imagine what she was thinking.

But that was part of the fun with Hannah.

Isn't that why you gave in to her demands so easily?

The woman should be a damn hostage negotiator. It was impossible to tell her no.

But she'd made a good argument. Being away from her would only make him want her more. He knew that now. This was best for him, but he wasn't at all sure it was right for her.

She'd promised to keep it casual, but there was nothing casual about their relationship. Will had had girlfriends in the past, although he'd never felt the same way with them as he did when he was with Hannah. She pulled him out of the hole he'd been hiding in, and she had given him a reason to want to wake up in the morning.

It had been a while since that had happened.

Even Rafe had noticed a change in him the past few days. He'd joked that Will laughed twice in one day and that was a new record. Rafe had promised it had been years since he had even smiled.

Was his friend exaggerating? Was Will really that unhappy before he met Hannah? He'd been in a dark place, but he hadn't realized how dark until now.

He texted Rafe to see if he'd heard anything about the investigation but his friend wrote back that he hadn't. He knew how important the clothing was to Hannah and he wanted to do what he could.

Hannah ran over to him and threw her arms around him.

"You are such a trooper. You didn't even fall asleep during the show."

"The things I do for you," he grumbled. But he finished the words with a smile.

"Now it's time for your big surprise," she said suggestively.

Will didn't care what it was. He'd follow her anywhere.

"I'M ABOUT TO TAKE YOU to the coolest club. You never know who'll be there, but you'll love it."

"I'm not one for the club scene, Hannah. I prefer quieter places."

She pulled at his hand. "Just trust me, old man. You're going to like this place. Besides, I thought marines were supposed to be like party dudes."

"I suppose some are. Officers have to set an example for their men." There was a hint of pride in his voice.

"So fun isn't usually a big part of your day?" She shivered against the cold as they moved down the street. Fashion outweighed survival most days and her bulky winter jacket was at the back of her closet. As they stopped at a red light, Will placed his heavy coat over her shoulders.

"You don't have to do that. I'm used to the cold." She sniffed.

"Sure, sure. That's why your teeth are chattering while you talk."

He had her there.

"As for fun, I don't know. I guess I don't think about it that much. My job keeps me pretty busy. I mean, I work out and play my guitar now and then. And I don't mind a good round of Texas Hold 'Em."

"Yeah, buddy. You are a real rebel." Hannah laughed.

"I'm going to infuse some fun into that life of duty of yours. Not that duty isn't important. It is. But so is life."

She glanced up to find him frowning. "I'm sorry. I've offended you in some way." What had she said? Was there anyone in the world with worse foot-in-mouth disease than her?

"Not in the least. I was just thinking about what you said. That's all."

She wasn't so sure about that.

"You didn't tell me it was a blues club." He stopped short at the top of the stairs leading down to the lounge.

"Well, when I borrowed your phone when mine didn't have service the other night at dinner, I saw you had your music on there. And I sort of peeked."

Will's eyebrows rose.

"I know, I know. You can probably throw me in jail for snooping. But I saw how much blues music you had on there. My friend Dickey owns this club. Master Z. is playing tonight. Dickey says he's one of the greatest blues guitarists of all time and I have to agree."

"He is," Will whispered as she yanked him down the stairs into the basement club. "Wait a minute. Dickey Meyers is a friend of yours? And the king of blues, Master Z., is here? Tonight? Are you serious?" Will sounded surprised.

"Yep. I met Dickey through my friend Kevin when Dickey was looking to upgrade his digs with some style. At the time I was still trying to get my name out there and took any job I could get. They came to me because Kevin likes my funky 'tude. And Master Z. is an old friend, as well."

"Is there anyone in this town you don't know?"

Hannah shrugged. "What can I say? I'm friendly. Bonky!" She fist-bumped the bouncer. He was a scary-looking biker guy on the outside and a big marshmallow on the inside, unless he didn't like someone. There was no way into the club, no matter whose friend you were, if Bonky didn't like you.

"Hey, there, little Miss Hannah. You got you a man tonight."

Hannah chortled. "Don't act so surprised, Bonky. You'll scare him off." She winked.

Bonky held up his hands in surrender. "No harm, *chica*. I was just thinkin' he was a lucky fella. That's all."

"Oh, that's a good save. Can you get Raymond to give us one of the good tables? My friend here is a big fan."

"Got it." Bonky pushed a button on his headset. "Hannah Banana is here with a military-lookin' dude. Tell the host to give her a good table up front."

Inside the club they stopped for a moment at the front desk where reservations were taken. Unlike most of the clubs in the area, Dickey's also served food. Nine years sober, he didn't like the idea of people drinking on empty stomachs. There were several people waiting in line but Raymond motioned her to come around the crowd.

"Ah, you look more beautiful every day." He kissed her cheek lightly. With his heavy Puerto Rican accent, he wasn't the easiest guy to understand but she adored him. She loved the whole gang here. When she was redesigning the place she'd come to know them all very well. And most of them treated her like a little sister. Except for Dickey, who called her the daughter he never had.

She hadn't minded a bit. He was caring and loving—unlike her real father.

"Aw. Don't embarrass me in front of my date."

Raymond looked behind her and threw a hand against his chest, spewing Puerto Rican so fast, even if she understood it she wouldn't have been able to keep up.

"I take it that means you approve?" Hannah couldn't help but laugh.

"*Sí.*" Raymond fanned himself as if he were flushed.

"No hitting on my date," Hannah playfully chided. "Take us to the table."

Raymond teased, "You never let me have any fun."

The club was casual with layers of blue, giving it a very insulated feeling. She'd taken the blues literally when designing the look of the place and even after two years she was proud of the work. There wasn't anything particularly elegant about it. Dickey wouldn't have approved, but there was a definite Rat Pack vibe with the dark colors and rich woods. The rounded stage jutted out into the middle of the room, hence the Blues Circle.

"This place reminds me of some of the blues joints I've been in. Only it's a lot classier. You did a good job of making it feel like the real deal without the grunge."

"Uh, thanks, I think." Hannah laughed.

The lights dimmed and Master Z. walked out onto the small stage. He hooked up his electric guitar to an amp and from the first strum Hannah could feel the music deep in her soul. A quick peek at Will and she saw he was in some kind of trance, his fingers following the rhythm on the table. The tension that always creased his brow eased.

It dawned on her that he was always at attention. He seldom let down his guard. The only other exception had been when they made love. She'd glimpsed the raw need in him that night—one that matched her own. It suddenly became her mission to help him relax more. If she had to seduce him to make that happen, she would.

Master Z. finished his set. As he walked off the stage he gave her a wink and made a hand motion that only she and a few others would understand. She nodded.

"What was that?"

"His way of ordering coffee." Hannah flagged down the waitress and gave her the order, adding a new round of drinks for she and Will and some nachos.

"Wait. He's coming to our table?"

"Yep."

"You know him?"

"Well, yeah. I told you I did. He was playing here when Dickey asked me to do the reno. I designed four jackets for him that he wears when he's out on tour with his band. This is home base. In fact, he lives in one of the apartments upstairs."

"I'm going to meet—" He stopped talking as the musician arrived at their table.

"Pretty girl." Master Z. kissed Hannah's cheek. "You come out on a cold night like this to see me?"

"Of course. And I brought someone who loves your music."

"Ah." Master Z. held out a hand to shake Will's.

"What branch of the military you in, son?"

"Marines, sir." Will shook the other man's hand. "How did you know?"

"You have that look about you and the posture. I've played a USO tour at least once a year for the last twenty years. I know military when I see it. So you like the blues?"

"Love it, sir. Love it."

Master Z. smiled. "You call me Z.—everyone does. No reason for formalities here. What's your name?"

"Will, si— Uh, Will." It was the first time Hannah had seen him flustered. There was even a bit of pink on his handsome cheeks.

"Do you play?"

Will nodded. "But not like you. Several men in my unit play and it's one of the ways we pass the time."

"Well, I got an extra set of strings back there. Why don't you join me for the next set?"

Will blanched and Hannah stifled a laugh.

"I'd be honored, but there are people here. I don't think I can do that."

"I don't follow you, son."

He motioned to the bar patrons around them. "These people came to see you. I don't think they'd appreciate my amateur playing."

"Well, I want to hear you play. How about you, Hannah girl?"

Will's beseeching look had no effect on her. Okay, it

did, but she knew if he didn't do this he would regret it for the rest of his life. She'd promised him a surprise, and this could possibly be the best one he'd ever received.

"I haven't heard him play, but so far he's good at everything. And I do mean everything." She waggled her eyebrows, and Master Z. hooted.

"Now that's a recommendation if ever I heard one. You don't worry about what those people think. I want to hear ya play." He sipped his coffee. "Come on. Let's find you some strings."

Will gave Hannah a look of horror as he stood. "Hey—" she grabbed his hand "—you'll be great. Trust me, all kinds of people come in here to play. People are used to it. And I have a feeling you aren't going to suck."

As he walked off, she thought his hands might be trembling a little.

12

WILL, WHO HAD FOUGHT in two wars and faced more enemy fire than he cared to remember, was about to throw up. How had he been talked into playing with one of the greatest blues legends to ever live?

He blamed Hannah.

"How does this one feel?" Master Z. handed him a guitar.

Will took it because he didn't want to be rude, but his mind was trying desperately to figure a way out of the situation. He put the strap over his shoulder and fingered the head of the guitar. That's when he realized what guitar it was.

"This is the one you played in New Orleans at the jazzfest concert."

"Were you there?"

"No, si— No. I was in Afghanistan, but a friend of mine videotaped your concert and uploaded it for those of us overseas. I can't tell you how many times I've watched it." Will squinted his eyes. Could he sound more like a psycho fan boy?

"Well, then, I want you to play it tonight. Seems fitting. Let's go."

The older gentleman tugged at Will's sleeve.

He reluctantly followed him out, keeping his head down to avoid the spotlight. An extra stool had been set up for him while they'd been backstage. After waiting for Master Z. to sit, Will did the same. Plugging his guitar into the amp, he waited.

The flock of birds fluttering in his stomach threatened but Will swallowed hard. He would not puke in front of all these people or one of his musical heroes. Master Z.'s music had helped him through some tough times and he would do his best to not embarrass the man.

Master Z. pulled a microphone closer to them. "This here is Will. He's a marine and he fights every day to keep us safe. Let's give him a hand."

Will's nerves intensified. What if they started throwing things when they heard how bad he was? He was going to kill Hannah for not helping him get out of this.

Master Z. strummed a few bars from an old John Lee Hooker song Will knew well. He let the music swell around him and without thinking his fingers joined in. He desperately tried to focus on the music and not think about who he was playing with on the stage.

After four minutes, which had felt like a lifetime, the music ended. The applause was loud and Will could see a few people standing. He figured it was the fact he

The Reader Service—Here's how it works:

Accepting your 2 free books and 2 free gifts (gifts valued at approximately $10.00) places you under no obligation to buy anything. You may keep the books and gifts and return the shipping statement marked "cancel". If you do not cancel, about a month later we'll send you 6 additional books and bill you just $4.49 each in the U.S. or $4.96 each in Canada. That is a savings of at least 14% off the cover price. It's quite a bargain! Shipping and handling is just 50¢ per book in the U.S. and 75¢ per book in Canada. * You may cancel at any time, but if you choose to continue, every month we'll send you 6 more books, which you may either purchase at the discount price or return to us and cancel your subscription.

*Terms and prices subject to change without notice. Prices do not include applicable taxes. Sales tax applicable in N.Y. Canadian residents will be charged applicable taxes. Offer not valid in Quebec. All orders subject to credit approval. Credit or debit balances in a customer's account(s) may be offset by any other outstanding balance owed by or to the customer. Please allow 4 to 6 weeks for delivery. Offer available while quantities last.

NO POSTAGE
NECESSARY
IF MAILED
IN THE
UNITED STATES

BUSINESS REPLY MAIL

FIRST-CLASS MAIL   PERMIT NO. 717   BUFFALO, NY

POSTAGE WILL BE PAID BY ADDRESSEE

THE READER SERVICE

PO BOX 1867

BUFFALO NY 14240-9952

Play the Lucky Hearts Game

and get...
2 FREE BOOKS and
2 FREE MYSTERY GIFTS...
YOURS TO KEEP!

yes! I have scratched off the gold card.
Please send me my **2 FREE BOOKS** and
2 FREE MYSTERY GIFTS (gifts are worth about $10).
I understand that I am under no obligation to purchase
any books as explained on the back of this card.

Scratch Here!
Then look below to see what your
cards get you...*2 Free Books
& 2 Free Mystery Gifts!*

151/351 HDL FJC2

FIRST NAME   LAST NAME

ADDRESS

APT.#   CITY

STATE/PROV.   ZIP/POSTAL CODE

Visit us online at
www.ReaderService.com

Twenty-one gets you
2 FREE BOOKS and
2 FREE MYSTERY GIFTS!

Twenty gets you
2 FREE BOOKS!

Nineteen gets you
1 FREE BOOK!

TRY AGAIN!

Offer limited to one per household and not applicable to series that subscriber is currently receiving.

Your Privacy—The Reader Service is committed to protecting your privacy. Our Privacy Policy is available online at www.ReaderService.com or upon request from the Reader Service. We make a portion of our mailing list available to reputable third parties that offer products we believe may interest you. If you prefer that we not exchange your name with third parties, or if you wish to clarify or modify your communication preferences, please visit us at www.ReaderService.com/consumerschoice or write to us at Reader Service Preference Service, P.O. Box 9062, Buffalo, NY 14269. Include your complete name and address.

was a marine. A lot of people had more respect for the armed forces, more so than they did in the past.

Will smiled his thanks and started to rise.

"Where you going?"

"Back to the table," Will told Master Z.

"Nah, you sit here and finish out the set. You're damn good, boy. You got some soul in them white-boy bones of yours. Probably seen more hurt than you should for a kid your age, but it comes out in your music. So sit your butt down and let's get going. Don't suppose you can sing?" Master Z. pushed the microphone toward him.

Will laughed. Master Z. had just called him damn good. He wished he'd recorded that. "I sing a little, but I think I'll stick with the strings."

The older man shook his head. "Nah, I heard ya hummin'. You sing this next one."

The giant frog that was lodged in his throat threatened to croak, but Will managed to get the words out. He closed his eyes and lost himself in the music.

Forty-five minutes later he was allowed to leave the stage. Master Z. followed him to the table after they put up the guitars.

"Hannah girl, you didn't tell me the boy could really play. And that voice..."

Hannah gave the man a thoughtful look and then faced Will. "That was mean good. Like, for real. Your voice is like nothing I've ever heard. So smooth, and you can play the guitar. You're a double threat."

Will waved her off. "Nah, I just make it look like I can."

"Bull. If I say you're damn good, you're damn good," Master Z. interrupted.

"You heard him say that, right?" Will's smile was so wide it made his face hurt. He probably looked like an idiot, but he didn't care.

"Oh, yeah. You are just full of surprises. People in the audience were even talking about you. In a good way," she added. "Master Z., you are the best."

"Hell, that boy can come back and play with me anytime. The way Dickey's looking over here, I have a feeling your military man could actually book some dates."

Will laughed out loud. For the first time in a long time he felt so free. He glanced down at his feet to make sure they were touching the ground. "Now you guys are laying it on a little thick. But thanks for the confidence. It'll be a good story to tell the guys in my unit. Though they're never going to believe it."

"Oh, they'll believe it." Hannah held up her phone. "I videoed it and took several pics. I already sent them to your phone and email."

Will was happy. He didn't care if he was good or if they were trying to make him feel better. It was a great night.

Master Z. stood. "Listen, I've got to get back to work. But I want you to have my email and phone number." He handed him a card. He wasn't sure what surprised him more, that the seventy-year-old man had email, or that he gave his personal address to Will.

"You want to get serious I'll hook you up with some guys who might be interested in recording you. Blues can always use an infusion of new blood and you've got the talent."

Will took the card and stuck it in his wallet. He stood up and held out his hand. "I want to thank you for letting me play. This is one of the best nights of my life and one I'm never going to forget."

Master Z. shook his hand. "I mean what I say. You can come play with me anytime. And also—" he pointed to Hannah "—he needs to meet Terry and Hawkeye. He's got a look and he can play that guitar. That voice of his is blues gold. They're going to love him."

Hannah smiled.

"You kids enjoy your date."

After he left, Will sat there for a moment. "I don't know whether to kiss you or kill you for that."

Hannah made a face. "Definitely kissing would be better. You were having fun up there. I could tell."

"I was, but I damn near puked before he started playing."

"I thought you looked a little green. But you know what? I think you surprised yourself and you certainly did a good job of surprising everyone in this place. I don't understand why you don't see how good you are."

This time it was Will who shrugged. "If you say so. Who are Terry and Hawkeye?"

"Record producers. Like he said, they are always looking for new talent."

Will chortled. "Record producers? This night can't get any weirder."

"They'd love you. Master Z. is right. You have that

whole hot thing going for you and you play as well as anyone else I've heard here."

Hannah picked up a nacho and bit into it.

He liked the fact that she ate like a real person. So many of the girls he dated in the past existed on salad and liquid shakes. Though with Hannah's energy, he figured she burned through calories like matchsticks on a bonfire.

"Boss wants to chat with your man," Raymond said from behind her. Will hadn't even seen him walk up.

"Well, tell him to come over. But if it's about him playing here, he's going to have his work cut out for him. Will doesn't think he's good enough."

Raymond waved a hand in front of his face. "Ludicrous. You're the best thing that's happened in here in a long time. I'll send the boss over."

By the time they'd left the club Will had promised the owner that he'd play when he came back to town. He couldn't believe everything that happened. And he owed it all to Hannah.

She might be chaotic and a little off-the-wall, but she was also one of the most incredible women he'd ever met.

"Your hotel is about six blocks that way." She pointed down the street as they reached the subway.

"I'd feel better if you'd let me take you home either on the subway or a cab. I don't like the idea of you going alone."

Hannah patted his chest. "I'm a big girl and I've been living in the city all my life, Marine. I don't need a bodyguard."

How could he tell her that he wasn't ready for the night to end? "I— Please. You've done so much for me tonight. Let me do this."

She gazed into his eyes. "You told me that you have an early day tomorrow. If you take me home, I'm going to drag you upstairs and make wild, passionate love to you. Are you up for that?"

Pretending to think about it for a minute, Will finally said, "I guess that would be okay. I mean, you did promise the possibility earlier in the evening." He said it dejectedly but couldn't hide his smile.

"Well, don't sound so happy about it. We could grab a taxi but subway would be faster," she promised.

"Subway it is. And you know I'd invite you to the hotel but—" Will wrapped an arm around her shoulders.

"No way. Too many prying eyes. I don't want your dad to know that I'm continuing my evil plan to corrupt the venerable Captain William Hughes." As she rubbed her palms together, she gave an evil cackle.

"Corrupting me?" Will tried to hide his smile. As if her sweet soul could compare to his darkened mass of nothingness.

She gave him a sexy look. "Oh, I have my ways, Marine. Trust me. You be nice, or I'll show you."

"Promise?" He pulled her close and kissed her hard.

Her cheeks flushed pink and he liked the idea that he caused the reaction. "Oh, yeah," she said breathlessly.

At her loft, she began stripping as soon as the elevator door closed behind them. She threw clothes off as she half ran to the bedroom. Will resisted the urge to pick them up. He unbuttoned his shirt as he followed her.

She was on her knees waiting for him, beautiful and naked, the moonlight giving her a not-of-this-earth quality, her waves of hair falling over her breasts. Her silky skin called to his hands to touch her. She was a gorgeous creature. His heart tugged at the sight of her eagerness.

She wanted everything to be free and easy. He'd agreed. But after tonight, the way she'd taken him to the club because she knew he liked the music... No one had ever done anything like that for him. Not that grand gestures mattered—it was that she cared enough to go to the trouble. And she'd encouraged him even though he'd been unsure. And she'd helped make a dream he didn't even know he was allowed to have come true.

She was a treasure. His treasure.

She clapped her hands. "You're thinking too much and you're too slow, Marine." She pulled his belt through the buckle and unzipped his pants. Her hand slid to his member and she pumped him through his boxers. Will managed to rid himself of the rest of his clothes before she slid her mouth up and down his cock. Her lips and mouth suckled and teased him, and he wasn't sure how much longer he could hold on.

"Hannah," he gritted through his teeth. "You have to stop. I can't...keep control when you do that." The last words came out as a grunt. She was wicked with her mouth. He'd never felt anything so good—well, except when he'd been inside of her.

She didn't stop and his hand slid down to pull her head back, but he found himself gently twisting her hair in his hands. Every muscle in his body contracted as he forced himself to hold on, but her tongue wouldn't stop. The tension below his cock was building and the sensation of her mouth riding him was more than he could take. He let go of her hair and stepped back. The cold air on his cock was exactly what he needed.

"Hannah," he begged her, his voice hoarse. "Please."

She lifted her head, her face full of innocence. "Please what, Will?"

"Stop." He put his hands on her arms. "It's your turn." He pushed her back and brought her hips forward to the edge of the bed.

"Will?"

He shook his head and knelt down so that his face was even with her heat. His tongue pushed hard at the nub there and he gently pulled her in with his teeth. She squirmed beneath him and her soft moan urged him on. His machinations continued, sending her into a frenzy.

"Will," she begged, her voice full of need. That he had such power over her body was heady, but giving her pleasure was the biggest high.

She hissed a breath and he saw her hands fist the sheets.

The third time she arched her back and screamed his name he caved. Standing, he lifted her legs and put her feet over his shoulders. Eyes at half-mast, she reached around so she could guide him to her.

Home. This was where he belonged. She met him

thrust for thrust, her hooded eyes never leaving his. A small smile on her lips was his undoing.

"Come for me, Marine. Come for me."

As always, he followed orders.

13

WILL STIFLED A YAWN and then smiled. He had exactly two hours of sleep before he'd raced back to his hotel to change clothes in time for his first team meeting of the day. They were in the conference room at the hotel, but would be heading over to the UN in an hour. Then he had his special team of attachés who would keep eyes on the American ambassador for a hostile Middle Eastern country.

"Sir?" Rafe stopped as he walked in the room.

"Lieutenant?"

"Uh…" The other man had a huge grin on his face.

"What?" The word sounded harsh but luckily Rafe wasn't someone who cared about his tone. Their friendship went deeper than that.

"I'd like to preface this by saying it's about damn time. But you need to lose the grin or your pops will find out what you were doing until the wee hours of the morning."

Will shot him an evil glare.

Rafe laughed loud.

"I don't care what he thinks, she's good for you. I've never seen you smile like that."

Will shrugged. His friend was right but the last thing he was going to do was share his feelings.

"I played the blues with Master Z. last night."

"Wait. What? Oh, hell, no." The quick change in subject caught his friend off guard.

"Oh, hell, yes. An entire set. H——" The general walked in with his team and Will couldn't finish the sentence. When his father looked his way, Will made sure he had his usual surly frown on his face. Rafe was right about that. He wouldn't dare let the old man see him happy.

"Marines, we have a problem. Captain, I think you're our go-to man on this particular subject."

Will sat up a little straighter. His dad seldom ever looked at him during these meetings, let alone called on him.

"Sir."

The general leaned back in his chair and crossed his arms. "Seems the ambassador and his family have some domestic problems. You're in charge of that team, so it's up to you to take care of it."

Will stared at his father. This was some kind of setup. He could feel it coming. Determined to take whatever came his way, he steeled himself. "I'm afraid I don't understand, sir. Are you saying that you need me to vet a new staff for their household? We processed the list yesterday and everyone checked out."

"No. That isn't it. I'm told the family's belongings

are on a ship somewhere in the Indian Ocean, with little hope of arrival anytime soon."

That happened a great deal, but the staff could easily replace anything the family wanted. Still, he didn't argue with his father.

"As you know, the family can't leave the compound and the ambassador's wife has made a request."

Will nodded.

"She needs a stylist. From what I understand that has to do with fashion, and given your latest escapades I thought you would be the right man for the job."

The general's men didn't bother to hide their snide grins.

Rafe's hands tightened into fists on the table. His friend always had his back.

Fine. The general wanted to dress him down in front of his peers. He could take it.

"Brilliant, sir." Will was surprised when his voice didn't crack. "I am exactly the right man for the job. I have people who would be happy to help. I'll get right on it."

The rest of it was worth it when he saw the frown on his father's face.

Two can play this game.

HANNAH AND ANNE MARIE ushered the last of the buyers out the door. Their day had been spent going through the designs with editors and buyers, and it had been an exciting day in so many ways. They had more orders than they could ever imagine.

"We're going to be so rich." Anne Marie fist-pumped the air.

"I have to admit that was epic." Exhausted, Hannah sat down at the conference table. It had been almost as stressful here in the studio as the show and they had three more days of this. "How are we going to fulfill these orders? It's at least ten times what we projected."

"You don't have to worry about it, remember. That is my problem."

Hannah put her hand on Anne Marie's. "No, it's our problem. You are doing a great job."

"I hear a *but*..." Anne Marie drew her hand away.

"No, but I do want to be more involved, that's all. I need to know what's going on here." She waved a hand around the room. "You'll still be in charge of making it happen. In fact I'm making you vice president of operations."

Anne Marie sat there with no expression on her face. "That's a really big title."

Reading the other woman was impossible. She thought her friend would be happy. "You're already doing the job and that of ten other people. You might as well have the title."

Hannah jumped up to grab her purse and from it pulled out a box.

"I had these made this morning and I forgot to give them to you."

Her friend opened the box. "Business cards?"

"Yes."

She ran a finger across the raised type. Hannah had ordered the best she could find and had them do a rush job. "Oh, my Gawd, this is so awesome." A grin spread across Anne Marie's face and Hannah was relieved. For a moment she thought her friend might toss the cards in the trash.

"I'm glad you're happy. Now tell me how we're going to make this happen."

"With all the buzz, I had a feeling we would have more orders than we projected. Our suppliers are ready, I've already interviewed potential staff and we're good. Seriously good. I've been working on a report just to make sure I have the planets aligned. I'll email it to you."

"You are a wonder, Anne Marie." Hannah smiled at her friend. "And you never fail to amaze me with your talents. I loved the way you covered the fact the sunshine blouse was missing by saying it was couture only. People were fighting over it. Oh, and if we have it in the budget I'd like to give Kathryn, Brenda and Jesse raises. I can't believe what they accomplished in forty-eight hours."

Anne Marie continued fingering the cards. Hannah was grateful her friend liked them. It seemed like such a small thing, and she should have done it long ago.

"I'll check the numbers to see where we are with the budget, but with all the orders we should be good. I guess now we are onto London. Do you have an idea of how you want the show to run? I have the specs from the venue."

Anne Marie glanced up. "I don't want to ruin a great moment but has Rafe or Will heard anything about the investigation?"

As much as she wanted the clothes back, Hannah hated that her friend still felt so responsible. "Nothing yet. Will talked to Rafe last night, but it will work out. You'll see." Hannah hoped her friend didn't notice the fake optimism.

Her phone rang and she saw it was Will.

"Sorry, it's the hunky marine."

"Well, pick it up." Anne Marie flapped her hand as if to tell Hannah to hurry and answer.

"Hi, Will, how are you?"

"Good." There was a long pause. "I need you."

"I'm here for you." Her voice sounded more suggestive than she meant.

He chuckled. "That's good to know. But right now I have a job to do and unfortunately that means finding evening dresses for the ambassador's wife and daughter for tomorrow night."

Hannah's jaw dropped. Will was out saving the world and they had him hunting down dresses? It didn't make any sense.

"We're on lockdown at the embassy. I can't tell you why, but the ambassador's family can't leave the residence."

What he didn't say was apparent to Hannah. The family had received some kind of threat.

"There is a special reception here tomorrow and we are tripling security. But the mother and daughter won't have the opportunity to shop as they planned. It was actually my father who asked me to contact you."

The general? Now that was just crazy.

"Will, as much as I want to help you there is no way I can design and make dresses by tomorrow."

"Oh, no. I didn't ask you the right way. I mean, do you know someone who would have those kinds of dresses all made up? And is there any possibility you could bring them here? We've already got you clearance."

Hannah's mind whirled. Leland could help her out. He had a huge warehouse of new and vintage designs. She had a few of her own, but it depended on what size they were. She wanted to do this. For Will, and the other reason was to show the general that she was a good person. She had no idea why that was so important to her.

He's Will's dad and you want him to like you.

She didn't have time to think about what that meant.

"Can you have someone text me their measurements? It's going to take me a few hours to pull several looks together."

"Hannah?"

Her mind was whirling with details of what she would need. Shoes, accessories. "What?"

"I'll owe you big," he said, the words as a whisper.

Her heart fluttered and her nether regions tightened with need. "Oh, and I'm so going to make you pay up, Marine. Just you wait."

THREE HOURS LATER Hannah pulled the van up to the gate and passed through security without incident. The Gothic structure of the building made it look like something on a street in Paris. The size of it rivaled her parents' Hamptons house and took up most of the block. Will and Rafe were there to meet her.

She wanted to hug Will but remembered he was on duty. No longer would she do anything to embarrass him.

"Hi." She waved to both of them.

Will gave her the sweetest smile. "You didn't have to do this but I'm grateful."

It was the least she could do after everything she'd put him and Rafe through. "No problem. I'll need help getting the racks out of the van."

"Sawyer and Rankin, help get these clothes out of the van," Will called to two men in uniform. His voice was authoritative and it made her grin.

This tough-marine side of him was a huge turn-on, especially since she knew ways to make him beg.

He collected her keys from her and walked toward his men. She couldn't hear what he was saying but he was there for a good minute.

"Okay, they'll take care of getting the clothes upstairs. I'm also going to have them replace your fuse, check the tires and fill it up."

"Will, you don't have to do all that."

"But I want to. Why don't you come with me and I'll introduce you to the ambassador's wife and daughter."

She followed him upstairs, grateful that she'd changed into her new leather boots and a wrap dress. Growing up around wealth did have its advantages. She knew when to throw her funky fashion proclivities to the wind and dress like a grown-up.

At least every once in a while.

When they reached a long hallway, he stopped and took both of her hands in his. He kissed her quickly on the lips. "I've missed you."

Those tender words launched butterflies in her stomach and her breath caught. The man could be so charming when he wanted to.

"I've missed you, too. You didn't wake me when you left this morning."

"You looked like Sleeping Beauty and it seemed like I'd be breaking some kind of law if I woke you. Besides, I left at five and I didn't think you would appreciate it."

Hannah placed a hand against his chest. "Will, that means you've only had a couple of hours of sleep."

"I sometimes go seventy-two hours at a time without sleep. Hell, I've been on assignments when I didn't get more than an hour over five days. Besides, every time I get tired, I think of what you did last night when—"

A door shut at the end of the hall and he stepped away.

"We should be careful here," Hannah warned. "I promised myself I wouldn't do anything to embarrass you further or get you into trouble."

"Are you afraid of my father?"

Hannah thought about it for a minute. "Isn't everybody?"

That made him laugh.

He led her to two double doors at the end of the hall and made the introductions. The ambassador's wife, Laura, reminded Hannah of a younger version of her mother, only she smiled more. The daughter, Regan, on the other hand, was a sullen mass of gloom. She barely raised her head from the book she was reading.

The dresses arrived on the two racks from her van.

Will excused himself, and she showed Laura, as the woman had insisted Hannah call her, the choices.

"You are a magician. I would wear every single one of these dresses. How did you know my taste so perfectly?"

Anne Marie had done an internet search on the wife and daughter, who had been photographed at several events. Thanks to her friend's efficiency, they had plowed through Leland's warehouse and boutique to find exactly what they needed. They had taken their cues on what to bring from those photos. She could tell Laura, but she liked the idea of being a magician. There was a certain magic in fashion. The right clothes could transform a person and even change a mood.

"I'm glad. I wasn't sure about your coloring before I arrived but I think the emerald green with the three-quarter-length sleeve would be a good start."

"That one caught my eye right away. I'll go change. Regan…" The girl didn't look up from her book.

"Young lady, you will respond when spoken to. Hannah went to a great deal of trouble to help us out. Now get up and find yourself a dress." Her tone was so much like Hannah's mother's, it was spooky. And it had about as big of an effect.

"Do not make me call for your father." The threat worked.

As the girl stood, Hannah realized she was much older than she'd looked in the pictures she'd seen. The photos had made her seem like a demure young girl. She had long black hair that fell past her shoulders and a heart-shaped face. She was model slender. For the first time she looked Hannah in the eyes. There was a rebel hiding in there somewhere. She'd seen that look many times in her mirror.

"I hate these parties." It wasn't so much a whine as a statement.

"I hear ya. When I was young my parents always made me make an appearance. Bor-ing. Snoozefests. I felt like some doll they were showing off. The hardest part of the whole night is trying to stay awake. Oh, no, the hardest part is pretending like you are paying attention and nodding at just the right time."

The girl almost smiled. "I'm not going to wear some dress that makes me look like a princess from an animated movie."

Hannah laughed. "That's good, because I brought everything except princess wear." Regan wore a pair of chinos and a sweater over a button-down cotton blouse. A very preppy look. But Hannah noticed her watch had skulls on it. A secret Goth locked in a preppy world. She probably wasn't allowed to wear what she wanted.

When she was younger, Hannah had run into the same thing with her parents. As long as they were paying for her clothing, she was expected to dress like a proper young woman. That was probably one of the reasons why when she began buying her own clothes she went more for funky whimsy than conservative.

"I didn't know your style but I brought several options. There's a black dress I think you might like."

The girl sighed. "My mother will never allow me to wear black."

Hannah smiled. "Well, we'll have to make her see reason, won't we? Besides, you might not even like it."

When she pulled the dress off the rack, Regan's eyes lit up, though her face was still in a frown.

"I guess I can at least try it." The girl almost grabbed the dress and ran to the sitting room next to the bathroom where her mother was changing.

The door to the sitting room opened and the ambassador's wife entered. Tall and sleek, Laura was ready to walk the runway.

"This is perfect. I would have searched for weeks for something that fit so well, and I still wouldn't have found it."

"It's beautiful." Hannah walked behind her and finished buttoning up the back. The dress had a high neck and a slit to the knee. It was sexy without being too provocative.

"Leland, a friend of mine, designed this. He does a lot of red-carpet dresses for movie stars and singers. It's a little big in the waist—if you want me to take it in, I can."

The woman shook her head. "No. It's nice to have some breathing room. It's appropriate, without being matronly. I may have to visit your friend when this business is done. Though, lately..." She sighed. "Sorry. I'm tired of being stuck inside. For several months there have been threats against Regan and myself specifically. We aren't allowed to go anywhere without a team of security, and even then, it's never anywhere public. I thought we'd be freer here but... I'm rambling. I'm tired of my own company. It's been so long since we've had visitors who weren't military or government personnel. There are those who are fighting for democracy where we're posted and my husband's support of that has put us in danger. Still, we'll persevere."

Hannah smiled. "I'm glad I could help. It's always fun to run into another fashion aficionado."

"I do love clothes. That's one of the great luxuries of traveling the world with my husband. Up until lately I could shop everywhere I went. So how did they convince you to come in today?"

"A friend of mine is working here and it's nice to understand that part of his job is keeping you safe."

"Would that be Captain Hughes?"

Afraid to reveal anything, she nodded.

"Ah, the captain. Yes. He's one handsome fellow. One of the few people in the house Regan will actually look at when he speaks to her. So is it serious between you two?"

She should deny it, but she didn't feel like lying. "We've both agreed that we're just having fun. What gave us away?" Hannah checked the hem of the dress. It did look as if it had been made for her.

"The way he looked at you when he left. That boy is taken with you."

She wasn't sure what to say to that. This was a quick fling. They weren't supposed to give each other longing looks or turn stomachs to jelly with sweet words, though it happened to Hannah almost every time they were together.

"I don't know…" Regan stepped in front of her mother so she could see herself in the full-length mirror.

The girl tried desperately not to smile, but Hannah knew she loved it. The bodice was fitted and the skirt flared. A tight jacket laced up the back. Slightly Goth but appropriate enough for the reception. The shoes would be the kicker.

"Well, you could wear black heels with it, which would be great. But I also brought these." Hannah found a pair of heeled lace-up boots that were replicas of the early 1900s style.

"Those are rather odd," Laura said.

"I love them." Regan held the boots as if they were spun of gold. "They're better than anything I could have dreamed. I need black tights."

Hannah reached into a bag. "Here."

Regan actually gave her a full smile and ran off to the sitting room again.

"I don't love that dress but I won't say a word," Laura said. "That child hasn't smiled in months. Of course, I can't say I blame her. We brought her home from the boarding school in Switzerland when the threats began. She loved it there and is furious that she isn't allowed to graduate with her friends. Now she feels trapped. If only she could understand we are doing our best to keep her safe."

"Can I ask how old she is?"

"She turns eighteen in three weeks. She plans to go to college this fall, but her father is worried about her safety. There are some religious zealots who have made multiple threats and they even went so far as to break into our home. They didn't get far, but the invasion made my husband even more paranoid. The consulate here agreed to put us up for a few months and we aren't sure what will happen after that. It's a tough way for a young girl to live."

That would be tough. "From the time I was sixteen until about twenty I don't think I ever smiled. I lived to drive my parents around the bend." Hannah still did. "They had certain expectations that I had trouble living up to." Hannah had no idea why she was sharing this information with a stranger. Perhaps because she understood how Regan felt. No one had been there to back her up, and maybe she could help the girl.

"My father finally gave up on telling me how to dress and he told my mother to do the same. He said if I wanted to experiment with my clothing and the color of my hair, it was better than drugs. He was right. I'm an artist and back then I needed an outlet."

Laura pursed her lips. "I butt heads with her, even when I try to be understanding."

Hannah laughed. "Call it hormones but I think girls are supposed to hate their mothers no matter what when they reach a certain age. And Regan doesn't hate you, but she feels stifled. That is what all the sulking is about. I don't know her well, but I was a lot like her when I was that age. You may not approve, but this dress is a way for her to show her true self."

The woman sighed again. "You may be right. Would you mind unbuttoning this?" Hannah did what she asked.

Laura passed her daughter but didn't say a word about the dress or the shoes.

"I heard what you were talking about," she whispered. "I don't hate her. I'm just tired of being stuck with no friends. They even read my texts. I had to open a fake email account to talk to everyone. It's embarrassing."

Hannah nodded. "You're old enough that you deserve some privacy, but they're only doing this because they love you."

The girl rolled her eyes. "That's why it's so hard. I'm scared, too, but I'm not going to spend the rest of my life like this." She turned to see the back of the dress. The detailed stitching on the back of the jacket was exquisite. "If it weren't for Jeremy being here I would go mad."

Laura walked out and hung the dress back on the rack. "Thank you again, Hannah. I hope you'll join us tomorrow night. I know it may be a boring affair but your young man will be here."

The last thing she had time for was a boring reception, but the look on Regan's face made her cave. "Thank you. I'd love to come, at least for a little while. I'm afraid I have to get ready for a London show, so if you see me leave early that's why." Why did she need to explain? She was busy. She didn't need excuses.

"I'll make sure you're on the list. If you would like to bring a friend, let Will know."

Hannah turned to Regan. "Do you ever wear your hair in curls?"

"Not since I was five." The sarcasm dripped.

The best way to drive a teen mental was to ignore their jibes, so Hannah did.

"If you do the sides up like this—" she brought the girl's long hair up "—and do curls down the back, it will show off the dress's neckline. That's how Red John had the models styled for the runway."

"Red John?" Regan pulled up the hem of the dress. It was a bit long.

"Yes, a new designer. He and I shared a stage a couple of days ago. My stuff is light and airy and his is dark. We're a good fit. He's also a great friend. We sort of bonded in design school."

"I can't wait to go to college. I've applied everywhere. But I have no idea what I want to do yet. My father and mother think I should have my entire life planned out by now."

Hannah laughed. "Well, even if you did have a plan, it would probably change. Though, I knew I would be a designer by the time I turned twelve. I hid my sketches for years. My mother was appalled by my chosen profession and my father thought it was flighty and irresponsible."

"So what did you do?"

"I went after my dreams and I didn't look back. Sometimes you have to take a risk now and then if you want to make things happen for yourself."

Regan nodded. "I like a boy," she said softly. "Jeremy, the one I mentioned, has been working with the chef here. He's a line cook, but he wants to be a chef with his own restaurant someday. Of course, we have to meet at odd times and only for a few minutes. He's asked me out on dates, but there's no way they'll ever let me leave.

"Besides, my parents would freak. He isn't the son of one of their friends. He actually works for a living. I'm so tired of the pompous asses they make me dance with at these parties. Rich kids with no personalities."

Hannah frowned. She understood needing to protect the girl but eventually she would jump out of the bubble. They'd never get her back once she did if they continued to restrict her so much.

"Jeremy sounds like a nice guy."

"He is, but he's not as hot as Will. I heard what my mom said. Man, you are so lucky. I saw his picture on your website. Hey, why didn't you bring your own designs?"

"My stuff is...well..."

"Wouldn't be appropriate for an embassy reception?"

"I have some evening wear that might work, but no, it wouldn't be appropriate for you or your mother."

"Well, I love this. Thank you." The girl turned and gave her a hug.

Hannah returned the gesture. She'd been Regan only a few years ago. It was hard not to like her, sullen attitude and all.

"Hannah, you're needed downstairs," Will interrupted.

A small giggled escaped Regan's lips.

Hannah cleared her throat. "I'll be right there." She turned back to the girl. "The dress is long in the front. Do you want me to shorten the hem?"

"I like it that way. It barely touches the floor."

"If you're sure. I'll come back early tomorrow in case you change your mind. And feel free to try on some of the other dresses. Oh, and here's my cell." She pulled a card out of her purse. "If you need anything. Clips for your hair or whatever. Let me know."

The girl nodded. "One thing. Why are you doing all this? You're a big-time designer, one of the top ten talents in the world. Don't give me that look. I read all of the articles about you."

Hannah shrugged. "I did it because Will asked me to."

14

"THEY'RE CALLING FOR a blizzard. I thought I should get you home." Will resisted the urge to touch her. His men and the household staff were milling about. Everyone had a job to do for the party tomorrow. Blizzard or not, the summit would happen, as would the reception to begin the event.

"What do you mean? I can drive in a blizzard. I've done it plenty of times," Hannah said. She had a confused look on her face.

"Yes, but if you drive yourself then I won't get to see you alone." He hoped she understood.

She started to say something and then stopped. "Actually I hate driving in the snow. I was giving you my tough, independent side. Letting you know I can take care of myself."

They both smiled.

Inside the van, they were quiet for a few minutes as Will maneuvered the vehicle onto the slick streets. The blinding snow made it nearly impossible to see and he was grateful to be the one behind the wheel. He would have been worried sick if she tried to drive in this. Hell, he wouldn't have let it happened.

"What happened today?" Hannah's question surprised him and he didn't know what she was asking.

"What do you mean?" Will's concentration was on the road.

"You said your father asked you to call. Is that true?"

"Do you doubt my word?" Will sounded almost belligerent but he didn't mean it that way. He wasn't used to people questioning his word. "Sorry. This snow is out of control."

"No, I'm sorry. I shouldn't have bothered you while you're driving in this."

Now he felt like a complete ass. Just like the general.

"My father tried to humiliate me this morning by announcing in front of everyone that he had a special assignment for me to find clothes for the ambassador's family."

"Oh, Will, that's awful."

Will smiled.

"That isn't the reaction I expected from you. I'm so mad at your father for doing that to you."

"It's great you have my back, but I handled it. I told him he did have the right man for the job and that I would take care of it. I acted as if I were excited about it. Shut him up and wiped the grin off his cronies' faces."

"Oh, I would have given anything to see that."

"Rafe probably took a picture," joked Will. "He's sneaky with the camera phone. The whole thing is kind of screwy. There are a hundred different people they

could have called to do this. And I don't think it was
the general's idea.

"Sounds like my mom interfering. She probably said,
'You had better be nicer to that boy. If he skips another
Christmas because of you, you're going to be eating
sandwiches for the rest of your life. I talked to Laura,
and they have nothing to wear. See if William can call
that friend of his.'"

"I think I love your mom."

Will turned up the defroster. "She's a great woman
and the only person who can handle my father. The
truth is, my dad isn't a bad guy. He's been through hell
and back. Up until I joined the marines, I idolized him.
And when he was home, which wasn't often, he was
a good dad—strict, but fair. But my joining the corps
changed all that. Something about thickening my skin,
I'm sure. So what about your parents? You mentioned
they weren't exactly happy about your career."

Hannah gave an unladylike grunt. "If my father
would let her, I would so be disinherited. I envy you
your mom. I think mine sees me as competition in some
way. The only way she can be happy is by making me
miserable. Of course, I don't help by pushing her buttons. But we all have our different ways of dealing with
the parental units."

When he neared her building she pushed the button
to open the small garage to the left.

"It's been a while since I've seen a blizzard like this.
Sandstorms, yes. Snow, no."

"Yeah. The last few years it seems like the snows

are getting worse. Do you have time for a drink? And how exactly were you going to get back?"

"Subway. I have a couple of hours. The team for the reception meets at nine. But I know you have a ton of work to do and helping out the ambassador's wife and daughter took a lot of your time."

"I still have to eat and I'd rather not do it alone."

Saying no wasn't an option. Every moment he could spend with her was one he would cherish. Part of him hated how much he needed her. Her life was a chaotic mess but it was never boring. And though she claimed to be a selfish rich girl, she had more kindness in her than anyone he'd ever met. Her smile was enough to make him believe there was goodness in the world, an idea he'd given up long ago.

"Will?"

He lifted his head and discovered he stood just outside the elevator door that opened directly into her apartment. "I'm preoccupied with work. Sorry."

She gave him a sweet smile of understanding. "I get that way. You worried earlier about pulling me away from work, but I needed the break. When I get too consumed I tend to lose focus. When I worked on Regan's dress today I remembered that I—" She stopped and rolled her eyes. "Doesn't matter. They have pizza downstairs. I've asked Anne Marie to bring some up. I hope that's okay."

"I like hearing about your work. I would tell you about mine if I could." He followed her to the kitchen.

"I understand. I didn't at first but I do now. I wish you could share the pain I sometimes see in your eyes.

Laura told me probably more than she should have about the people who are after them. She and Regan are so lonely, but they both understand what is going on.

"You're doing an important job, Will, and so is the ambassador. They've made such strides in that country and the actions of a few could cause an international incident that would make it difficult for everyone there." She poured the beans into the coffee grinder and pushed the button.

In a way he was glad the ambassador's wife had shared part of the story with her. But he could never tell her about the pain she mentioned. That would torture them both.

"I can't imagine anything happening to Laura or Regan. You are going to keep them safe, aren't you?"

Will's fingers caressed her cheek. "They are my team's priority."

He wanted to tell her the ambassador had assembled a great security team of his own, but after the breech at the embassy a few months ago they knew someone was compromising them from the inside. Part of Will's assignment, one Rafe didn't even have a clue about, was to find out who that was.

"You're doing it again." Her fingers clasped around his. "You don't have to stay. I'm the first one to understand about duty. Though, I have to admit I haven't done such a great job of it lately."

She moved so that she was next to him and she wrapped her arms around his neck, pulling his head down to hers. When her lips captured his, he felt as if he was home again. A dangerous thought crossed his mind about making this permanent but he forced himself to concentrate on the kiss.

"Hey," she said against his lips. "You're thinking too much. I don't have any expectations. I'm good with the moments we share and grateful for each one."

He tucked his knuckle under her chin. "I was thinking the same exact thing a few minutes ago. I want to make promises to you, but I don't know if I can keep them."

She backed out of his arms and ran a hand through her hair. "I'm not going to lie and say those things don't cross my mind, too, but neither of us can make promises. You have your life and I have mine and they—" She took a deep breath.

"Pizza is— Oh. Am I interrupting? You said you were hungry." Anne Marie held up two boxes.

"Starving," Will said, giving Hannah an extra few seconds to compose herself. He took the pizzas from her friend. "I would have come down."

"No prob." Anne Marie looked at him and then Hannah and then back to him. "Is… Uh…"

Will shook his head in a warning.

"So, Will, any news on the investigation?" Anne Marie changed the subject.

"Not yet. Tag and his team have some leads they are following up on. Rafe tells me these guys are the best at what they do. Hopefully, we'll hear something soon."

"Great. We appreciate you guys getting involved." Anne Marie pursed her lips. "So…I'll be downstairs if you need anything else."

Hannah kept her back to him.

"I didn't want to upset you. I should go."

Her shoulders lifted as if she were breathing deep again. "No. I want you to stay as long as you can. But I meant what I said before. We keep this easy. We enjoy each other's company. I leave in a week for London and you'll be gone, too."

He put a hand on her shoulder. "That doesn't keep either of us from wanting more. But you're right. We can't count on the future. So I say we eat pizza and get fat."

She turned into his arms then. And gently poked a fist into his belly. "I think you'd have to eat a whole lot of pizza to get fat. Me, on the other hand, more than two pieces and I'll have to work out two hours every day for two weeks. It isn't fair."

"You'll always be perfect to me." Will meant the words. She was gorgeous but even when she was old and gray he couldn't imagine feeling any different about her. He squeezed her tight. They might not want to admit it out loud, but she was his. And he was hers.

"Let's eat."

HANNAH HAD HOPED they would at least have time for a quickie but shortly after they finished the pizza, Will received a phone call that sent him back to the embassy. The blizzard was insane, but he'd texted her to let her know he was safe.

Earlier, when he mentioned promises, so many possibilities flashed through her mind. Over and over she explained this was a fling, but for her it was so much more. She'd never met a man who turned her inside out.

The strength and power within him thrilled her when he was near. When they made love it was as if their bodies were in perfect sync. There was no thinking or awkwardness, only feeling.

Part of her was angry with him for helping her to realize there could be so much more in a relationship. Now she knew sharing your soul with someone you cared about was the most satisfying experience ever. When they parted it would kill her.

Of that she was certain. But she would be strong for him. As far as she was concerned he would never know that her heart had been broken into seven million pieces. When he'd mentioned the promises, it had seemed like foreshadowing what it would be like when they parted ways.

Shattered. That was the right word. She knew it was coming, but she was determined to spend every moment she could with him.

Hannah picked her sketchbook off the table in front of the couch. Her work would be her only solace when he went off to war again. She would write him emails and even letters if that were the only way he could communicate. She would pretend all was well and do her best to keep him company while he fought so far from home.

You're thinking about a future with him.

Shut up.

Tension tightened her jaw when she considered a future without Will. Her mind pushed at the thought that once he left, he might never come back again.

Hannah's pencil broke against the pad.

The buzzing of her cell phone pulled her from the heartbreaking thoughts.

"Hey, it's Will."

The guy must be psychic.

"Is everything okay?"

"Everything is fine here, but I thought of something."

"You're going to have to give me more details," she said.

"We were doing a last-minute update on the guest list and going through their security clearances. For some reason it triggered something. You know those women, the ones in the corner you called the Hags?"

She had no idea where he was going with this. "Yeah."

"Two of them stopped Jesse and Anne Marie that night as they were taking out the clothes. I'd been watching you talk to the press. I turned to pick up my hat and I saw them. It was just a glance so when I saw them at the party it didn't really register. But at the party there were three of them, and only two were backstage."

"Are you saying you think they took the clothes? Why would they? The other one probably had gone to another show or something."

"That's the thing. The one that wasn't with them fits the body type we saw perfectly. I'm not sure why I didn't see it before."

"But they aren't even designers. Why would they do something like this?"

"No, but they might have connections to those people who mass market the clothes. And you said they were wannabes who failed and then began to criticize. What better way to get back at an industry that made them feel like fools? It's absolutely diabolical."

Thoughts jumbled in her head and her mind had a difficult time switching gears.

The Hags as black-market thieves?

"Okay, say they are involved somehow. How do we prove it?" Hannah sounded skeptical.

He's trying to help you. Quit being a jerk.

"Sorry. I'm just really confused."

"Well, this came out of the blue, so I can't blame you. Rafe has already called his friend Tag. They are contacting Jesse and Anne Marie as we speak to see if they remember anything suspicious about the conversation that night backstage."

"Oh. Okay."

"But there's more. I told you about the task force a couple of days ago. Turns out there have been long-term investigations into couture—that's a word I never thought I would say—thefts and some of the bigger fashion houses who kept having their designs stolen only to find them manufactured and on the street in a matter of weeks. Until now, none of their leads ever panned out. You guys may have helped them big-time with this case if the Hags pan out."

"Oh," she said again. She couldn't seem to form words. The Hags? Really? She tried not to hate anyone, but Hannah had a difficult time thinking any kind thoughts about the women.

"Those horrible witches have been spewing hate while they snuck into some of the best couture houses and stole the very things they snarked about. Oh, I want to punch them. No, I want to get in my van and mow them over until they are flat pieces of mascara goo. Yes. That would make me happy," she said through gritted teeth.

Will chuckled. "Now don't hold back, hon. Get it all out."

"You have to understand how I feel right now. Oh, my Gawd, if this is true the entire industry will be up in arms. They'll be lucky if they live the next forty-eight hours. We are all so proprietary about our designs. I want to shoot them. You're a marine—you have a gun, don't you?"

Will made a strangled sound over the phone and she had a feeling he was trying not to laugh.

"It isn't funny."

He cleared his throat. "You are right. The situation isn't funny at all. But trust me, Tag and his men will take care of those horrible women."

Will had done this for her. Once again he'd solved a problem so huge she didn't know how she would survive it. She wanted to hug him right then. The strength of his arms wrapping around her and holding her tight would be heaven. She hadn't admitted it to anyone but she'd been sick about part of her first collection being ripped off. It wasn't about the money; it was more an issue of pride. She'd been so proud of achieving her dreams and then she had them ripped from her in a matter of hours.

Tears rimmed her eyes. Will had done it again, swooped in and saved the day. "It wasn't us. You did

this, Will. Bless that observant brain of yours. I'm…
It… Uh…"

"Are you all right?"

The last thing he needed right now was to worry about her. "Oh, yeah. This is so weird. I'm having a tough time wrapping my mind around it. They would be the last people I would suspect, and it's like karma is having a giant field day."

"You sound strange. Do you need me to come back?"

Hannah forced herself to smile so that she would sound happy on the phone. "You have a big day tomorrow. I'll be fine."

"So there *is* something wrong."

Her elevator doors opened and Will stepped through.

"What— How did you get up here?" She spoke into her cell and then stuffed it in the pocket of her jeans. "You should be working. And the storm."

Will didn't say anything. He was across the floor and had her in his arms.

This was where she belonged. The strength emanating from him seeped through her, helping her to find an emotional balance.

"Life is hard sometimes," she whispered.

He guided her to the couch and pulled her onto his lap. "Tell me what's going on in that mind of yours." He pointed to her forehead.

"Right now, it's like a ping-pong match using twenty balls at one time. There's the stolen clothing. The new show in London. The buyers have been coming out of the woodwork— I can't believe I just said that. It sounded like something my dad would say."

"All but one of those things is good and that problem may be solved, too."

She ran her knuckles across his jaw. He probably had to shave twice a day to deal with the stubble. "Yes, but it's a lot to handle all at once. We're a fairly small operation. I don't know how we're going to fulfill all the orders we have and get ready for the show. Don't get me wrong. Like you said, these are good problems to have. It's scary for me. I've realized I have to grow up. I can't keep dumping everything on Anne Marie. She already has her hands full."

"Hannah, you've got great people working with you. Trust them. And you've got Rafe and me. We're going to get the people who stole your clothes."

She kissed his jaw. "It isn't fair."

"What?"

"That you're so handsome and smart. How do women resist you?"

"You promised we were going to keep this simple. There's only one woman who matters." The intensity in his eyes sent a small shiver down her spine.

"Is it simple? I can't stop thinking about you."

"No, it isn't simple. I feel the same way about you. The reason I was sad, even with the happy news, is that I didn't have you here to reassure me. It frightens me that in such a short time I've come to count on you for comfort and strength. But neither of us is in a position to— Our worlds are so— You may have to go off to—"

"War."

She couldn't acknowledge the word. It was too painful to think about.

"That's what scares you the most?"

She stared up at the steel girders in her loft, unable to speak. He'd nailed her worst fear and she hadn't even acknowledged it until then.

"You care that much?" He had the nerve to smile.

"Yes. I don't want to, but I do. The idea of losing you gets to me. And I am the *wrong* woman for you."

He laughed. "How can you say that? You're nearly perfect."

She snorted. "You and I both know that is so far from the truth. You need someone who is calm and keeps her emotions in check. I'm a neurotic freak show. Look at what just happened. I had a complete meltdown and my life is better than it's ever been. You need someone sane."

"You don't think *I'm* a freak show?" Will leaned back on the sofa and she didn't like the distance he put between them. She wrapped herself across his chest.

"No, you're strong and so solid. And beautiful. And you are one of the kindest men I've ever met."

Will grunted. "Hannah, I'm not kind. Do you have any idea what I've had to do the last eight years? There are stories I could never tell you because they are so disgusting. Memories I'm going to have to live with the rest of my life. Some nights I wake up in a cold sweat. It isn't pretty."

Hannah wrapped her arms around his. "Do you want to talk about it? I would listen. I whine a lot, but I'm a lot tougher than I look."

He chuckled. "You are a blessing, a warm lamp of light that has lifted my soul the last few days. Hell, you've shown me that I still have a soul. I have to shove those things on a shelf, Hannah. I see a shrink regularly. You should know that about me. Almost all the men in my unit do. We see, not to mention do, some pretty ugly things and it can be tough on the psyche."

She turned so that her knees surrounded his thighs. "You're so hard on yourself. I'm glad you can talk to someone. I bet your poor shrinks have to have shrinks. It isn't fair what you have to go through in a day. And look at me, I'm here griping about stolen blouses and skirts."

Will gently touched her cheek. "I'll admit, a week ago, I would have said fashion was silly. But I've seen how much joy it can bring. I saw Regan in that dress. It's the first time I've ever seen her smile. You did that for her. Bringing joy is in some ways even more important than what I do."

Hannah rolled her eyes. "Don't even go there. But I want you to know something. I'm sure you have to be a superhero when you're on assignment, but with me…"

"If you call me that wuss Clark Kent, I'm so out of here."

She laughed and kissed his jaw. "I was going to say more like Wolverine. You're so protective, and normally the protective thing would bug the heck out of me, but I like it when you do it. I feel safe when you're around."

Will frowned and she thought back over her words. Maybe he didn't like Wolverine.

"Hannah, I lied before." He shifted her so that she was back on the couch.

"You're scaring me. If you're married, I'm so going to punch you."

"Really? That's where you went with this conversation? Uh, have I ever given you any inclination that I would do something like cheat on a wife?"

She frowned. "You have a point. I'm sorry. I had a run of cheaters a few years ago and that's when I sort of swore off men."

Will took a deep breath. "I think I'd rather not know about the men in your past. The idea of someone else touching you, making love to you, is enough to make me want to put a fist through a wall. I told you I had a temper. I keep it in check, but..."

"Noted. No old-boyfriend chat. Trust me, no one I've ever dated is worth remembering. Now what did you lie about?"

There was a long pause.

"I care about you. The kind of caring that isn't going to stop when you go off to London. I've pretty much known that since the first day I met you."

She had to be honest with him. He deserved it. "I care, too." She sighed. "Too damn much. I can't help it. We're stupid for thinking this could be some easy kind of fling. What are we going to do?"

A grin spread across his face. "You care about me, too?"

"Hell, yeah. Of course I do. I told you that earlier this afternoon. More than I've ever cared about anyone." Her hand went up to her mouth. She'd revealed too much. She didn't want to put any pressure on him.

Will pulled her hand away. "I feel the same way. We

just met, but I would do anything for you. Hell, I think I have."

"So what do we do?"

"I'm not sure. I've never really believed in fate but you running into me on the street has made me wonder. We've only known each other a few days but I'm having a hard time imagining my life without you now. What do you think about that?"

Hannah grinned mischievously. He was definitely on the same level she was in this relationship. It was bonkers. Beyond reason and common sense for them to even think about taking it any further, but she didn't care.

He lifted his eyebrows. "It scares me a little bit. But I'm a marine. I can handle it."

"Well, that's good, then. When do you have to go back on duty?" She began unbuttoning his shirt.

"Not until five tomorrow morning."

She plucked the phone out of her pocket to check the time. "That gives us nine hours. Let's make the most of it."

He scooped her up and carried her to bed. "Yes, ma'am."

15

REGAN TWIRLED IN HER DRESS, looking every bit a Goth princess. Hannah held up a hand for her to stop, so she could check the dress's hem. She'd arrived three hours before the party to make sure the clothing fit and that there wouldn't be any need for alterations. They were in one of the guest rooms, which had been assigned to Hannah. It was elegant and the perfect place to get ready for the reception.

"That looks better and you have less of a chance of ripping it with those boots." Earlier, Hannah had forced the young girl to walk around the room in the dress and Regan had nearly tripped more than once.

"Do you think he'll like it?" Regan followed Hannah to the vanity mirror where a fat curling iron waited to put curls in the girl's hair.

"Who?"

"You know—Jeremy. He helped prep all the food for tonight and he'll also be working as one of the waiters. I mean, it's stupid for me to worry about a guy liking what I wear. But tonight is important to me and I want to look—" she paused for a moment as if she were sizing up Hannah "—hot."

"Of course you look hot. I'm styling you. I wouldn't let you go out looking like some dweeb marshmallow. And if Jeremy doesn't see that dress as hot, he's gay. There's no other answer."

The girl laughed out loud. "He doesn't kiss like he's gay." Regan gave her a coquettish grin.

"I'm just messing with you. He'd be an idiot if he didn't like it. You look gorgeous."

And she did. Hannah had shown Regan how to make the most of her features with makeup, but didn't allow the girl to overdo it. The dress was enough of a statement.

Besides, she had a feeling Laura wouldn't go for a thick line of kohl-black liner around her daughter's eyes. The dress flattered the girl's figure and even Hannah was surprised by how stunning she looked. After finishing with the curling iron, Hannah placed a few sparkly clips on the sides to draw it up underneath.

"Wow!"

"You got that right." Hannah smiled at her in the mirror. "Heads will turn tonight when you make your way down those stairs."

Regan's smile fell. "Not for me. My mother will be beside me. She's so gorgeous that no one ever notices me. But Jeremy thinks she's old, so I might have a chance with him."

Hannah chuckled to herself. "Tonight, they will be looking at you, trust me. Maybe I should give you some

Mace to keep in your purse just in case Jeremy gets a little too excited.

"Hey, don't make a face. You look hot. And a girl has to protect herself. Boys just can't seem to keep their hands off of pretty things."

Regan rolled her eyes. "Stop or I will die of embarrassment."

Hannah had a feeling that for all her bravado, the girl had lived an incredibly sheltered life. "Why? Didn't you guys talk about this at your boarding school?" If Jeremy did show an interest, the girl needed some kind of sex education. Though, Hannah knew it really wasn't her job to do so.

"Uh, we talked about boys. Who was cute when it came to celebrities and stuff like that, but it was an all-girls' school in Switzerland. They are so strict it is insane, but it was better than— Anyway, there were some girls who said they slept with some of the boys in town. They would share stories, but we never knew if they were telling the truth."

"Do you need me to—"

"No!" Regan nearly shouted. "Trust me, I've had the sex talk at school and with my mother."

"Good." Hannah was relieved the talk wouldn't come from her. "You're almost eighteen and I figured you had, but if you ever have any questions... On second thought, I don't mind being your fashion mentor, but I'm the last one to give advice about relationships."

They both laughed.

Someone knocked on the door.

"Come in," Hannah said.

Will entered wearing a white shirt, dark blue suit and tie. The suit fit him across those broad shoulders. A perfect specimen of a man, and as of last night he was hers. A slight tremor zinged through her body when she thought about their lovemaking. It had been so tender and passionate, as if they were giving themselves to one another as gifts. It was a night that would keep her going during those long months when he would be gone.

His eyes met hers, and her heart sped up again. Dear heaven, he was gorgeous. Yes, he would definitely make a great model with his rugged chin and those high cheekbones. Hannah would never get enough of the man.

When he saw Regan, his eyes flashed in surprise. "Wow!"

Regan laughed out loud. "I know, I'm hot. Hannah said so."

"Well, Hannah would know. Regan, I've been asked to escort you to the den where your parents are waiting. They wanted to introduce you to some of the guests before you go downstairs."

The girl stilled. "My dad is going to flip when he sees me but I refuse to change. If he doesn't like what I'm wearing, then I'll stay in my room."

Hannah gave her a slight shoulder bump. "He might surprise you." After talking with Laura again, Hannah felt certain the ambassador had been made aware of the situation. Laura had explained that she and her husband would accept their daughter's fashion choices. She'd agreed with Hannah about the clothes being a form of expression. Laura had even shared stories about her punk-rock days in England. It was hard to imagine the sophisticated woman with spiked hair. Laura was the epitome of class.

"Captain Hughes, you stay here with Hannah. I can find my own way." Regan's chin lifted but she turned to smile at Hannah.

"Sorry, I have my orders. Besides, I'm looking forward to the look on their faces when they get a load of you." He smiled at the girl and she blushed.

"Hannah, you are welcome to come with us, or if you wish, the party has begun downstairs." When he spoke to her, his tone was formal. This was work Will. He'd explained to her the night before that while the reception was going on he had to stay alert and be all business. He wouldn't be able to visit with her. They had to play it cool because the general would be around and Will needed to focus.

Hannah didn't mind because when he looked at her the desire was there in his eyes. She had no business being at the party. In fact, it would probably be better for both of them if she'd stayed home and worked. But Will was here, and she'd made a pact with herself that anytime she could be in his presence, she would. Even if she couldn't touch him, like tonight, she'd be near. It was enough. She would also feel guilty if she didn't keep her promise to Regan. The girl needed to know that she had a friend on her side.

"I'll go downstairs. I don't want to interrupt a private family moment. But you guys have to tell me what happened later." She smiled at Will so that he would know she understood her place.

"Well—" Regan put her hands on her hips "—it's never private. Mom and Dad always have friends over. I think Will should stay here and kiss you."

"Regan!" Hannah admonished. "It's one thing to talk girl talk, it's quite another when the guy is in the room. Besides, Will is working. We both should respect that."

"I'm not going to tell." She crossed her arms and glanced up at Will. "Aren't you at least going to tell her she's beautiful? She looks like a model. I think she's even prettier than my mom, and that's saying a lot." Regan's shy side seemed to have left the building.

Will grinned at the girl. "Anyone ever tell you that you're a bossy brat?"

"No. But I'm about to change that," Regan said bravely. "I'm not going to be shoved into a corner anymore."

"Well, certainly not in that dress," Hannah added.

"You guys can change the subject all you want, but I'm not walking out of here until you at least tell her she's gorgeous." Regan continued to stand with her hands on her hips.

Will gave a heavy sigh as though it was a great deal of trouble to cross the room and put his arms around Hannah. "You take my breath away," he said as he kissed her lightly. "I can't wait to get you out of that dress," he whispered for her ears only.

"You look kind of hot yourself, Marine." Hannah grabbed a tissue from the vanity and wiped the evidence of their kiss off of Will's lips.

"Kind of?"

She pointed a finger at him. "You know how hot you

are. Now go save the world, and don't worry about me. I spent my life going to these things. I can handle it."

Will brushed his fingers along her jaw. "I'll see you later."

"Oh, you most definitely will," Hannah said suggestively.

Will crossed the room and stuck his elbow out to Regan. "Miss, may I escort you to your parents' preparty festivities?" His voice was formal and at the same time he had the sweetest look on his face.

The young girl wrapped her hand around Will's arm. Then she glanced back at Hannah. "I'll take good care of him. I promise."

They all laughed.

Hannah watched them go through the door and then turned to fix her lipstick.

He was so sweet to the girl. Will's compliments helped to give Regan the confidence she needed. He and Rafe always seemed to know the right thing to say to put other people at ease. She could use some of that. Hannah had a tendency to open her mouth and promptly insert her foot.

As she took one more glance in the full-length mirror, Hannah's heart skipped a beat when she remembered his words about what he would do with her dress later.

Yes, he always knew exactly what to say.

You might be working hard tonight, Marine. But you have no idea what I have in store for you later.

16

"MOM, WHAT ARE YOU doing here?" Hannah's breath caught in her throat. Had she fallen into one of those alternate realities? Or maybe this was hell. That was it. She must have slipped on her way down the stairs and she was dead. It would be preferable to the look in her mother's eyes.

They stood near the stairs leading up to the second floor. The foyer, living and dining areas were filled with chatty, elegantly dressed partiers. The ambassador was connected. There was no mistake about that. But her parents?

"I'm here to support the ambassador's wife, Laura, who is working with one of my charities. Why are *you* here?"

Ugh. Her mother always had a way of putting Hannah in her place.

"Hannah, is that you? My, you look lovely this evening." Her father smiled at her.

He wasn't around much and he didn't approve of her

lifestyle, but she never doubted her father's love. She couldn't say the same about her mother.

"Thank you." She stood on her toes to air-kiss his cheek, as she knew his dislike for lipstick stains on his face.

"I was inquiring as to why Hannah is here." Her mother gave her another pointed glare.

"I invited her," Laura said as she walked up. "She's a talented young designer and she is a trooper when it comes to a crisis. Our luggage was misplaced and we were...too busy to shop. Hannah took time out of her extremely hectic schedule to help us. She dressed Regan and myself, this evening. And she made us both very happy, which isn't easy to do."

Hannah's mother smiled at the other woman. "How brave you are to have someone like Hannah style you." Her mother could be such a bitch sometimes. In her wildest dreams, Hannah's mother would never deem Hannah worthy of dressing anyone above a prostitute. That was what she'd said the last time they'd discussed her career.

"I'm not at all sure what you are implying, Olivia. Are you saying you disapprove of my dress?" Laura looked skeptically at Hannah's mother, clearly waiting for a response to her question.

Hannah genuinely loved this woman. There weren't many people who would even consider challenging her mother.

"Not at all, I was just telling Stella Wellington that you must have a picture of Dorian Gray in your attic because you look younger every time we see you."

Her mother's words sounded so heartfelt, the ambassador's wife probably believed her. But Hannah knew the truth. Stella was as mean-spirited as her mother. More likely they'd been spewing hate with their vicious gossiping. She'd bet money on it.

Laura put a hand on Hannah's shoulder. "The lovely Hannah is the reason I look and feel so splendid. She's like a breath of fresh air. How do you know her?"

Oh, this was getting good.

"She's our daughter," her father said proudly. "Did you know her designs were the talk of the town the other day? The women at my office couldn't stop raving about her."

Hannah took a deep breath. For the first time in her life, her father approved of her. And he'd paid attention to her work.

"I must admit we haven't always been as supportive as we should have been. But she made it on her own, which makes me even more proud of her." Her father gave Hannah a genuine smile.

Part of her wished she didn't crave her father's approval, but she was grateful.

"Thanks, Dad," Hannah managed to squeak out.

He patted her cheek. For him it was like a bear hug. She would take it.

Her mother cleared her throat. "If you'll excuse us, we really must go say hello to the Meyerses. Lovely party, Laura."

"Did you say Hannah?" Another woman stepped into the semicircle before her parents could leave.

"Yes, Elisabeth," Laura answered. "I'm so happy you were in town. It's been ages since we've chatted."

The two women hugged.

"China was the last time. I still haven't forgotten that afternoon in the market. Best tea I've ever had," the woman named Elisabeth said.

Hannah didn't know who the other woman was, but she instantly liked her.

"Ah, yes. We always do find adventure, don't we?" Laura winked at her. It was if they were old school chums. "So have you met the lovely Hannah? She's the new It Girl of the fashion scene here. These are her parents, Olivia and Todd Harrington."

Her parents each held out a hand, as did Hannah.

"Oh, are you the one dating my son?"

"I'm sorry?" Hannah was confused.

"I don't think Laura mentioned my last name. I'm Elisabeth Hughes. William is my son. I believe you two are an item."

Her parents gasped.

Yes, Hannah was most definitely in hell.

DISTRACTIONS WERE THE last thing Will needed. Standing at the top of a stairway overlooking the party below, he surveyed the room. His team had been specially selected to cover embassy security for Ambassador Ramkin and making sure everything ran as smoothly as possible was paramount. Earlier in the day, there had been a fasle bomb threat at the United Nations, which meant everyone was on high alert.

The ambassador had insisted they carry on with the

reception. He didn't want the extremists to cause any disruptions with the upcoming summit. Will was in charge of all interior security and the embassy guards were stationed at all points of entry and around the property.

As Will glanced at Hannah for the hundredth time that night, he cursed the ambassador's wife for inviting his dream girl to the party. Tonight the fun-loving, miniskirted girl with cowboy boots was gone. In her place was a sleek uptown woman draped in a form-fitting sapphire dress that sent his senses reeling. He'd forced himself to stay away from her as much as possible so that he could focus on the task at hand, but it wasn't easy. What bugged him was he wasn't the only one looking. A variety of men had asked her to dance and Will didn't care for the jealousy that stirred within him.

She was his.

If he said something like that to her, she'd probably never speak to him again. It was one thing to discuss old boyfriends—it was quite another to have men trying to work his woman. He sounded like a possessive idiot, but he couldn't help it. More than once he'd sent Rafe to escort the men away from her using one excuse or another.

The one thing that kept him sane was that he had caught her stealing glances at him every few minutes. When their eyes met, she would smile knowingly and look away.

Her back was to him now and he wondered what it would feel like to run his hands down her spine to the soft cushion of her hips. The sounds she'd made the night before when they made love still rang in his ears. His body stiffened and he once again tried to gain control. He forced himself to shift his gaze and his eyes raked over the room in search of trouble.

Something about Regan, the ambassador's daughter, bugged him. The girl was twitchy. There was no other word for it. She kept glancing around the room as if she were searching or waiting for someone. He watched as she moved to a corner near a plant. A waiter walked up to offer her an appetizer and she smiled. He couldn't blame her for flirting with the young boy; there wasn't another person in the room near her age. She could be a brat at times, but he wondered if perhaps she was just lonely. He knew a little something about that having grown up with a father in the marines and moving every few years. Sometimes it was every few months.

In the few days he'd been around the family, Regan had always been off in a corner reading. He knew from her file that she was tutored because of the threats and she hadn't been allowed to be in contact with any of her friends. It was a horrible way for a young girl to live, but necessary in order to keep her alive. There was a mole, and until they found the culprit, no one in the family would be safe.

He'd never seen her smile until he walked in on Regan and Hannah earlier. That sweet woman of his had a way with people. Before he opened the door, he had heard them laughing. She was so full of joy and light, and she didn't even realize what she did for other people. She'd called herself selfish. Ridiculous.

He glanced back to Hannah, and his breath caught. His mother was talking to her.

Oh, hell. This can't be good. His mother had a way of wheedling information out of people. There were times when the general had compared her to Mata Hari. As a kid, he'd never been able to get out of anything. His mother had some sixth sense about those things.

After the grilling she would receive, Hannah might never speak to him again. He couldn't blame her a bit. The ambassador's wife seemed to be amused, but there was another couple standing with them. The woman looked as though she'd been sucking on a giant lemon. There was something familiar about her, but he couldn't place where he'd seen her before.

He pulled out his handheld computer and searched through to see if he could find the couple's names. When he did, he nearly dropped the device over the banister.

Hannah's parents were with his mother. And Hannah was caught in the crosshairs. From the look on Olivia Harrington's face she was far from happy with whatever was going on down there. How could a woman so bitter-looking be Hannah's mother?

More than anything, Will wanted to go down and save the woman he cared about from whatever drama his mother had created. His mom would never mean to cause harm, but she wasn't aware of Hannah's difficult relationship with her parents.

Damn. I should have paid more attention to the list.

He'd seen the Harrington name, but he hadn't put it

together with Hannah's. She would think that he had known all along and possibly kept it from her.

He had to get to her, but leaving his post was not an option.

Why did this have to happen now? His mother hadn't been on the list he had received when they were first vetting the guests. Rafe took care of the second round and probably hadn't thought it important to tell Will. His mother and the ambassador's wife were great friends. He should have guessed she would show up. But he hadn't been thinking clearly.

The idea of having Hannah near had overruled all logic. He hated how right his father had been.

This was the last thing he needed. Talk about distractions. Will forced himself to look away from his mother and Hannah and redirect his attention to the rest of the room. He had a job to do and he couldn't allow his personal life to interfere. He'd ask for Hannah's forgiveness later. In fact, he knew exactly what he would do to her to make her scream forgiveness.

His eyes continued the search.

The ambassador was speaking with a congressman, and two men to their left were watching them carefully. The men were eavesdropping, though they hid it well.

"Team B?"

"Sir," Rafe answered. They had set up four-man teams and Rafe was heading one of them.

"Two men to the left of the ambassador and the congressmen."

"On it," Rafe said. A few seconds later he was back on the comm. "They are activists from Shelride. Johnson has them covered. He's right behind them. Says he's been following them most of the evening. Doesn't like the blond, who keeps talking about how they spent all this money on a party when people around the world are starving."

Will frowned. "Tell him to stay on them. Bring the rest of your team to the floor."

"Yes, sir."

"Team A, what are you seeing on the cameras."

"Outside clear. Kitchen and surrounding rooms clear. We have eyes on the room. There's one blind spot near the plant to the north of the stairs."

That's where Regan had been a few moments earlier. He glanced down and the girl was gone. His eyes zeroed in on the room as he quickly scanned it, searching for her. She was nowhere in sight. She'd probably gone to the ladies' room, but it was his job to know her whereabouts at all times.

"Anyone have a twenty on the ambassador's daughter."

No one answered.

"B team?"

"We're on it."

One of the activists was also gone.

Will's gut churned but his mind went straight to work. He stayed in position watching the room as the teams searched the residence.

"Sir, I checked the ladies' and her bedroom. Nothing." The head of Team C was Lieutenant Carter, a woman who had become like a sister to him and Rafe. She was the only woman in his unit in Iraq, and she held her own with the rest of them. In fact, her quick actions, along with Rafe's, helped to keep Will alive the last time he'd been shot.

"Check with the guards to see if anyone left in the last five minutes. Shut everything down and don't let anyone out."

"Something is wrong. I can tell by your face." Hannah was next to him.

He'd lost it. There was no way anyone could ever sneak up on him like that. He had to get it together.

"Have you seen Regan?"

She shook her head. "Not in the last few minutes. I've been busy with— Wait. What?"

"She's missing."

His comm crackled. "We can't find her," Rafe warned.

"Damn."

"What is it?" Hannah reached out to touch his arm. "Is she okay?"

"I have to go. They can't find her anywhere on the premises."

"Oh, no. I'm coming with you."

Will took her hand in his. "We'll find her. I promise I'll call you later."

He took off in a slow jog down the stairs but stopped. He didn't want to draw attention to himself, as the party was in full swing. If someone here had taken her, he didn't want the person to know they were aware of the situation. The ambassador was speaking to the general. From the look of their conversation his father was already aware of what was going on. The ambassador had a tight frown.

The responsibility of losing the man's daughter weighed heavily on Will. The fact the general had seen the failure wasn't something he would soon forget. He could never quite seem to get it right when it came to his dad. No time to beat himself up. He had to find the girl.

In the kitchen the rest of Team B surrounded Rafe.

"No one saw her leave, sir," Johnson said. "None of the cars have left the valet lot. There hasn't been anyone in or out since the alert went up. Cameras didn't pick up anything. Whoever did this is a pro. They knew exactly where all the cameras were. There are maybe four blind spots and we had those all covered."

"Excuse me." Hannah stood in the doorway of the kitchen. "I think I know something that might help."

"Hannah!" Will couldn't keep the frustration from his voice. "I told you we're working here."

Her hands went to her hips. "Yes, and you think Regan's been taken, but I would bet big money that she's run off with her boyfriend."

"Boyfriend?" The ambassador was behind her and she moved into the kitchen to let him in. Will's father followed close behind.

"Yes, sir. When I fitted her dress she told me that he was the only real friend she had here, and she was asking me a lot of questions about relationships. She's been sneaking around so she could see him. And they've been emailing on a secret account."

Will glanced around the room. Everyone stared at her as if she had three heads.

"I know this is serious and that you have to check out everything. But you might start with the boyfriend. That is all I'm saying."

"My daughter wouldn't take off on her own. She's a responsible young woman." The ambassador's tone made Will feel sorry for Hannah, but it was her own fault. She needed to let them do their job.

"I don't mean to be rude, but she's an eighteen-year-old woman who reads romance books like she breathes. And if you check her movie-streaming cue, you'll find nothing but romantic movies. She probably thought you would be so busy with your guests tonight that you wouldn't notice if she snuck out for some fun."

There was a long silence.

"If it were you, where would you go?" the general asked Hannah.

"That I don't know—maybe to his place? He was working here tonight. I saw her talking to him earlier. I thought she might introduce us since she feels safe with me, but there's so much security she was probably afraid."

"The waiter," Will returned. "I saw her talking with him. We have everyone's IDs in the computer."

"On it, sir." Rafe's fingers flew across the keyboard. "Here are the photos." He turned the laptop toward Will.

As they scanned the photos, Will saw the waiter. "Jeremy Glenfield. Lives in Brooklyn. Let's go."

"I'm coming with you," the ambassador said.

"Sir, we don't know she's there. It's best if you stay

here in case we're wrong," Will warned. "We should treat this as a real kidnapping. We have no proof that she left on her own accord."

"Young man, she's my daughter and I'm coming with you. Your men can forward the call to me if one comes in. Do not share this information with my wife until we are sure what is happening. Is that understood?" the Ambassador said to the group.

Hannah's eyes narrowed at Will as he left. He couldn't blame her for being angry with him. He'd thought she was interfering at first, not offering help. Even worse was that it was his father who believed her first. He had a feeling he'd pay for that later.

HANNAH DIDN'T BOTHER to go back to the reception. Furious with Will, she had had enough. That he wouldn't give her a moment to explain infuriated her. As if she didn't appreciate how important his work was. Then he'd made her look like an idiot in front of Rafe and the rest of the people in the kitchen, including his father.

Men are stupid. She grabbed her coat from the woman who had checked it near the entrance, and headed outside. The weather had been horrendous, so she'd taken a cab to get there. Now she needed another one to get home.

"Ma'am, I'm sorry, we're in lockdown. No one can leave the premises." One of the guards at the door put a hand on her arm.

Hannah took a deep breath. "I know Captain Hughes." At least for the moment, she thought bitterly. "I have the beginning of a migraine and I feel quite ill."

It wasn't a lie. She was beyond pissed at him, and her head was banging like a kettledrum. "I really need to go home."

"I'm sorry—"

"She's okay. I checked," the other guard interrupted.

"Thanks." She gave him a grateful smile. "Do you know how I can get a taxi?"

"We'll take care of it," said the guard who'd tried to stop her.

The security men at the door arranged for one to pick her up outside the gate. Thankfully, the sidewalk heading to the street had been shoveled, but that didn't keep her from sliding in her six-inch Louboutins and landing flat on her butt.

"Ma'am, are you all right?" One of the security guards from the gate ran toward her.

"Careful. It's slick right—" she tried to warn him as he slid to a stop a foot away.

He held out his hand.

"Thanks." She gave him a tight nod.

"You're the captain's woman." He smiled.

His woman? She knew it was just an expression but still it bothered her. Right now she didn't feel like Will believed in her at all. "He's a friend," she said as he helped her up.

"We got a kick out of those pictures in the paper. It was kind of nice to see him having some fun. I saw him smile the other day when he was talking to you on the phone. I don't think I've ever seen him do that. Even with Rafe, and he's his best friend. He's always so serious."

Hannah thought back over the past few days. He'd smiled a lot when he was around her. They had a couple of moments that were tense but for the most part it was easygoing.

"Can I ask you something?"

The marine had offered his arm and she took it as they walked the last few feet toward the cab.

"Yes, ma'am. Anything."

"How many men are in your unit?"

"My direct unit is thirty men—well, there's one woman—but the captain commands over a thousand most days. We lost about twenty in a special team he put together to save some Iraqi women in a shelter a few months ago and he really took that hard. Insurgents bombed the place while the captain and the men were shuttling the women to the buses. It was bad. Captain Hughes also took a couple of bullets to the shoulder but he never stopped. He didn't leave a single man behind, even when he had to—" Abruptly the marine stopped.

"What?" The gunshots explained the scars she'd seen.

"Ma'am, it's not right to talk about that stuff in polite company. Captain Hughes will reprimand me for saying what I have. I've got a big mouth."

"Please, I want to know."

"If he finds out I told you, I won't be worth knowing."

"What's your name?"

"Private Scott, ma'am."

"I promise you, Private Scott, that I will never say a word about what you tell me tonight. I swear it."

He eyed her warily.

"Please," she begged.

"Even though he was injured, he ordered the bus to go on. Then he and Rafe, along with the remaining marines, picked up the pieces and made sure everyone was identified when they were brought back to base."

The pieces of men.

Hannah blinked back tears. It felt as if her stomach was slowly inching its way toward her throat. She heard about the horrors of war all the time, but Will had lived it. The man had suffered two gunshot wounds and still he wouldn't stop.

"He's a good man. Refused to quit. That is until he nearly passed out and the lieutenant forced him down so the medics could do their job. There isn't a one of us who wouldn't die for him. Just today, there was a threat to the ambassador and here we are safe and sound, thanks to the captain. He's what being a marine is all about."

Opening the door of the cab, he ushered Hannah inside.

"Private Scott, thank you for telling me and thank you for everything you do."

"It's our job, ma'am. You stay warm." He shut the door.

Hannah gave her address to the driver. It wasn't long before the tears fell and there was no way she could stop them. Here she'd been angry with him for not taking her seriously, but this was a guy who dealt with the worst the universe had to offer every day of his life. For all she knew he could be right about someone taking Regan. She hadn't been that worried before, but now she was.

Will had been short with her, but only so he could do his job in the most efficient way possible. If she'd been smart, she would have asked to speak to him privately for just a few seconds.

No. That probably wouldn't have worked, either. She wasn't sure how she could have made the situation better, but she felt certain she was right about Regan. The boy was gone, too, so her instincts screamed that they were together.

She hoped her gut didn't fail her this time.

17

WILL SAT UP WITH A JERK. The nightmare was back. His men blown to bits before his eyes. Heart racing, he forced himself to inhale slowly. When his phone rang, he jumped.

Easy there, Marine.

He checked the ID of the caller and answered.

"Rafe? It's five a.m. I've been asleep exactly two hours. This had better be good."

"I have a way for you to make up with Hannah."

Will wished he weren't so interested. He'd hated the way he treated her but he'd only been doing his job. A girl's life was at stake and there wasn't time to waste on guesses. Though, of course, Hannah had been right on the money. Damn. He owed her. "Tell me."

"Tag and his officers found the clothing. They made a significant bust. Seems these Hags you were talking about weren't so careful about hiding the stuff. Tag found the warehouse where they were storing everything and then played one against the others to get full confessions out of all of them."

Will smiled. "What happens with the clothes?"

Rafe grunted. "There's a small catch there. The clothes are in evidence and will be for the next forty-eight hours. Then Tag says they can be released."

"Tell Tag I said thanks. And Rafe…"

"Yes, sir."

"Thank you for calling in the favor and for what you did for the girl last night."

"No problem. So are you heading over to Hannah's?"

Will was a marine and could go for days without sleep but he was exhausted. "Soon," he said.

He lay back against the headboard. Marine or not, he was a chicken. He didn't want to face the disappointment Hannah must feel about him. She'd been right about everything. And there was no way they would have found Regan so fast if she hadn't been following her intuition.

"That's one hell of a woman you've met. You might want to keep her happy," his father had warned him last night after they found the girl safe. "She has a good head on her shoulders and a successful business. You could do worse."

That was as close as his father would get to admitting he approved of Hannah—something he didn't think would be possible. His mother had also gone on for more than half an hour about how impressed she was that a lovely girl like Hannah could have survived her parents' obvious dislike of her chosen profession.

"I don't like to talk rudely about anyone, but that

mother of hers. I mean, it's hard for me to believe Hannah is related to that woman."

She had a point.

But he'd blown it big-time.

Running a hand through his hair, he knew he could never go back to sleep. He had to talk to her. To touch her. To smell her. He was off duty for the next twenty-four hours. Once the summit began he didn't know if he would even have time to see Hannah before he shipped out again. Was he really going to waste time he could spend with her because he was afraid she was mad?

Thirty minutes later he stood outside her building in an old sweater and jeans. His bomber jacket was covered in snow but he didn't care. He thought about using the code he'd seen her punch in, but it was early morning and he didn't want to scare her by just showing up in her penthouse. But before he touched the panel, the door buzzed open.

After locking the door again he waited as the elevator churned its way to the bottom floor. When the doors opened, Hannah threw herself at him so hard he had to lean against the wall for support.

"I'm so happy you're okay." She wore a hoodie and sweatpants and her hair was a wild nest on top of her head.

"Why were you worried? You were right about everything."

She lifted her head off his chest. "I'm glad, but I also realized you could be right. I worried about your safety."

He squeezed her tighter and sniffed her sweet

vanilla-and-honeysuckle scent. The warmth of her was something that would never grow old.

"Trust me, that kid Jeremy was more than happy to turn her over to her father. He had no idea how complicated his life was about to be, but he was a fast learner."

"So much for true love. Is Regan okay? She must be crushed." Hannah stood on her toes and kissed his cheek.

He started to put his lips to hers but stopped. Shifting, he carefully moved away from her.

"She will be fine. Though, she cried most of the way home. She refused to ride in the car with the ambassador. He'd given her and the boy a hard time. Rafe and I took her in our vehicle and he told her that all men were toads. That she would have to kiss a lot of frogs to find a Prince Charming and that Jeremy was definitely a frog.

"The tears stopped about halfway home. She asked Rafe if he was a toad and he told her yes. Sometimes he was. Then he made frog sounds and she started laughing. Like I said, she'll live. I think she might have the beginnings of a crush on him."

"You guys seem to have a knack for saying the right thing at the right time."

"Not always." He held her shoulders. "I have to apologize for the way I treated you last night."

She pursed her lips. "The way I see it, you were doing your job. You didn't know she'd confided in me." After the look she'd given him last night, this was not the response he expected.

"Yes, but I should have taken you more seriously from the beginning."

She tugged on his hand and led him into the elevator. "I'm just glad Regan's safe. I bet she's really mad at me right now."

He chuckled. "No, you're in the clear. No one ever said a word about you being the one who spilled the news. She assumed we had been watching her. Evidently, they'd only been in the boy's apartment ten or fifteen minutes.

"In fact, she was upset that you'd left by the time she'd returned. She wanted to thank you for the dress and I think talk to you about her boy troubles. I feel sorry for that Jeremy kid. She let him have it for not standing up for her. I've spent the last three days looking after that family and I've never seen her go off like that."

"She's a punk girl hiding behind a preppy facade. She was bound to jump out of that shell at some point," Hannah said as the doors opened.

Will followed her into the apartment. "There's something else."

Hannah sat on the couch and motioned for him to sit down. That's when he noticed the shadows around her eyes.

"Hey, did you get any rest? Come to think of it, how did you know I was downstairs?"

She crossed her legs and put a pillow in her lap. "I've been on a creative binge. Desk's by the window and I saw you. What's the other news?"

"They found your clothes."

She jumped up suddenly, sending the pillow to the coffee table and knocking the wineglass that had been there onto the floor. A maroon stain spread across the white rug, but she didn't seem to care.

Will sprinted to the kitchen in search of some towels or a cloth but only found a roll of paper towels. He quickly blotted the spot.

"What are you doing?"

"You spilled your wine. It'll stain your rug."

She took the towels away from him. "It's okay. Don't bother."

He didn't understand how she could stand to let the stain spread and his look must have said it.

"Okay, okay. I'm blotting, Mr. Neat-nick. Now tell me who stole my clothes."

"Technically, I shouldn't as it is a pending case but it was as we suspected—the Hags."

Hannah sat back on her knees. "I don't believe it. Those bitches."

It was the first time he'd heard her use language like that and it was kind of cute.

"They've all confessed and it looks like they're involved in some messy international trade issues. They may be spending a long time in jail." He frowned. "The catch is, the clothes are in evidence. They have to keep them for forty-eight hours."

Her smile had enough wattage to light the room. "I'll have them in time for the show." She pumped a fist. "We would have had the new ones made by then, but now we can focus more on the new designs. What a relief. Anne Marie and Jesse are going to be so happy."

Will watched as she blotted the carpet. The stain would take some heavy-duty cleaner. He would find her some later in the day.

"What's wrong?"

She shook her head.

"Hannah?"

He drew her up off the floor with the paper towels still in her hand. "Hey, why are you upset?"

A tear fell to her cheek. "A lot's happened in the last few hours. That's all."

"There's more to it than that. Tell me, please."

Using the heel of her hand she shoved the tear away. "No. That's all."

Whatever it was, she didn't want him to push. "You're exhausted." He guided her from the living room to the bedroom, tossing the dirty paper towels into the trash bin. Neither of them had slept much. "Let's get you into bed."

"Can you stay?" she asked as she climbed into the bed fully clothed.

He pulled the comforter up to her chin and walked to the other side. "Yes." He stripped down to his boxers and climbed in bed. Wrapping his arms around her, he shifted her so that her head was on his chest.

"We should—"

He squeezed her tight. "We will. Later."

She yawned and snuggled against him. His body had an instant reaction but he shifted so she wouldn't feel it.

Before drifting off to sleep Will understood something that should have shaken him to his core, but it didn't.

He loved Hannah.

18

"WHAT ARE YOU DOING?" Hannah stood near the curtain that hid her bed from the rest of the loft. The news was on the television, but the sound was so low she couldn't hear it. Will was on his hands and knees doing something to her carpet.

"I bought some rug cleaner and I almost have the stain out." He didn't look up. The muscles under his T-shirt bulged and Hannah's breath caught.

"Coffee is made and I picked up gluten-free chocolate croissants for you. Anne Marie told me they were your favorite."

Her hand flew to her hair. "It's so late. I've missed the buyer appointments this morning."

"Calm down. Everything's been rescheduled because of the weather. Seems New Yorkers don't like walking in the snow. Can't say I blame them. I'm used to the desert heat myself. Oh, also I reorganized your linen closet and cleaned your kitchen. I hope you don't mind."

Mind? "You don't need to do this. I have a woman who comes in once a week. She'll take care of it."

"You have a maid? But you live by yourself."

"Will, you really are OCD, aren't you?"

"Yes, that is one of my many freak flags as you like to call them. The doc says it's my need to control the environment around me. And honestly, I like to clean. I like things tidy. I always have. Probably has something to do with growing up in the military."

Controlling his environment. Hannah could see why he would need to do that. When he and his men went out on their missions, there was only so much they could control.

The visual pictures from Private Scott's comments flashed through her mind. She forced herself to take a good hard look at Will and she recognized what an inspiring human being he was. And he cared about her.

Of course, she couldn't say any of that to him then. They'd just got back on an even keel—last thing she wanted to do was rock the boat. They had such little time left together.

"Well, I'm not going to stop you, if you actually enjoy it. I wish I were the same way. You should know that one of my freak flags, in addition to being a flighty flake, is that I'm kind of a slob. I've been known to leave my clothes on the floor for a couple of days when I'm really busy."

"Why do you call yourself a flake?" She noticed he didn't mention anything about her being a slob. The dishes she'd dirtied the night before were gone and her pad, pencils and sketch paper were neatly stacked on the bar.

"Um, I am. I have a tendency to go off on the creative binges and I forget normal daily-life things. Half the time I don't notice the messes I create. If it weren't for Anne Marie tracking my every move, I'd forget appointments and goodness knows what else. Even with her doing it, I still miss stuff from time to time. And I'm habitually late. I'm trying to change, though."

Will walked into the kitchen and put away the cleaning supplies. Then he washed his hands. "You're a creative person. I thought artsy people didn't really believe in time."

Hannah sat down on one of the bar stools and grabbed a napkin and croissant from the bag there. "Two months ago, I would have agreed with you. But I think it's more about immaturity and a need for control with me, too."

He opened her fridge and took out the few condiments, milk and coffee she kept in there. She noticed he'd also bought some deli meats and cheese. Poor guy probably couldn't find anything to eat that morning. What must he think of her?

"In what way is it about control?" He dampened a cloth and started wiping the inside of the fridge.

She stifled a chuckle. Now he was cleaning her fridge and she didn't even think he was aware of how weird it was. The poor guy had been through enough crap. If cleaning a fridge made him feel good, who was she to argue?

"Being late is about making people think that my

time is more important than theirs. It's rude, really. I'm sure many people aren't punctual all the time, but it's a real problem with my mother and her crowd. They are all about being fashionably late. I say I'm trying to get better, but then I showed up almost an hour late for the party Leland threw me the other night."

"Yes, but you were working. You'd just finished with the press when you had to wait for me to change clothes. That's not the same thing."

"Don't encourage me, Will. I'm really bad about it. The other day with your dad was the first time I'd been on time for an appointment in years."

"Really? So why then?"

Hannah had to think about that. She didn't have much time to get ready that morning. In fact, she'd set a personal record. "It was for you."

Will stopped his cleaning parade in her fridge. Turning, he gave her the strangest look.

"What did I say?"

"It's sweet that you did that just for me."

Her eyebrows shot up. "Yeah, well, don't get used to it. I hear it's really hard to break bad habits. By the way, are you going to clean all day, or do you have time to kiss me?"

"Oh, I always have time for that." He tossed the rag on the counter, then leaned across the bar to kiss her. His lips were soft against hers.

"I want more," she whispered.

He broke contact and the next thing she knew he was around the bar, pushing her thighs apart and pressing himself into her. "Like this?" He trailed kisses down her neck.

"Yes," she encouraged him.

His fingers followed the path of his lips. Lifting her shirt over her head, he suckled her nipples.

"Ummmmm. Yes." Grabbing his head, she nestled him between her breasts.

His hand found her heat, through the thin silk panties she wore. She was glad she'd changed into the long T-shirt earlier.

When his two fingers plunged into her, she gasped. Bucking against his hand she begged him not to stop. As he pumped her, Will drew her nipple into his mouth. The roughness was her undoing.

"Ooh." She screamed and her body started to orgasm.

He shoved the panties aside and plunged himself inside her. "Harder," she begged. Pounding so hard he moved the bar stool, he put his hands on each side of the chair to hold it down. Hannah scooted to the edge so he could plunge his shaft farther into her.

"Ride me, baby," Will grunted. She met every thrust.

Their pace was edging toward her breaking point. She locked her gaze with his. The passion and ecstasy there threw her into the best orgasm of her life. He wanted her. Crazy Hannah. He didn't care about her hang-ups. Or that she was a flake.

"Hannah," he whispered against her lips as he continued to move faster and faster inside her.

"Me, too," she said. Biting his lip softly she ran her tongue against it.

"Hannah," Will moaned again as he emptied himself inside her.

Body shaking, she hugged him to her.

Her Will.

She might have to say goodbye soon, but she was never going to let him go.

SOMETHING SUBTLE had shifted in Will's relationship with Hannah. It happened while he made love to her in the kitchen. He saw it in her eyes. She'd cared about him before, but it was more now. Could she love him? They hadn't known each other long, but he'd loved her from the moment they met. He knew that now—corny love-at-first sight and all.

But it didn't feel corny with Hannah. This thing between them was deep and real, and they both understood the stakes were higher now. It was obvious neither of them was ready to say the words out loud, but it was there.

He loved her. He would do anything for her, including changing the life plan that had been so carefully set before him. His father might never speak to him again. His mother's heart would break. But for once, Will wanted to plot his own path. Be his own man. Allow himself to do what he wanted.

He'd forced Hannah to go downstairs to her studio and catch up with Anne Marie, who'd called several times that morning. He knew why Hannah was hesitant to leave. He'd promised he'd be there when she was done.

He sat on the couch and turned up the television.

What the hell did he want to do with his life?

Could he really leave his men behind?

Hell.

That was the kicker. He would always be a marine through and through. Maybe his father had pushed, but Will had loved the life—at least until the past two tours. Losing good men always ate at his soul, but it was more than that. Had he lost the edge that made him a good marine? He liked to think he could make the tough decisions, but he didn't know anymore. And he dreaded the next tour.

His men deserved more. But giving up the corps?

The very idea turned Will's stomach.

Hannah needed him, too. She didn't realize how much, but she would. Her life was about to take off in ways she hadn't imagined yet. When he'd been downstairs earlier Anne Marie had showed him all the newspaper articles and features. Hannah was on her way to great things. But she would need to be surrounded by people who cared about her, who loved her. And no one loved her more than he did.

For the first time ever, his life was a mess. The plan didn't seem so clear now.

So what the hell are you going to do about it?

19

HANNAH JUMPED IN the cab with Anne Marie. It was her friend's first trip to London and she had been talking nonstop about it. As they neared LaGuardia, Hannah had to squeeze her eyes tight to keep from crying. This should be one of the happiest times of her life. Her first London show was several days away. There were hundreds of designers who would kill to be where she was.

I am grateful. She said the mantra over and over.

And she was.

Except for one thing. She didn't get to say goodbye to Will.

Filling her lungs, she took a deep, cleansing breath.

"Are you excited, too?" Anne Marie asked.

Hannah didn't trust herself to speak. She didn't open her eyes, but she nodded. She refused to whine. First, she was afraid if she did, she might never stop. And second, she didn't want to ruin her friend's enthusiasm.

It almost felt as though she'd left her heart somewhere. No more Will. His tour would begin soon and she might not see him for months, possibly years. It was hard for her to think of it.

"I can't believe…" Anne Marie began.

Last night Will was supposed to have come over and they had planned to say their goodbyes. But a security breach had him stuck at the United Nations and he hadn't been able to leave. Rafe used Will's phone to text her to explain.

The captain is furious. I don't think I've ever seen him this mad. But turns out the threat was coming from the ambassador's own security team. The captain has several men left to interrogate. It doesn't look good.

She asked Rafe to tell Will she understood. And that she would miss him. Maybe he could call her in London if he had the time.

But the text had depressed her deeply. She hated that she'd grown to need him so much and she cared more than she ever thought possible.

Before last night, she'd planned how she would say goodbye to him. She would make sure she had his favorite meal and that they made love until they were so sated they could barely breathe. Then she would lay atop him soaking up every bit of his strength to tide her over in the months to come.

Then she'd received the text.

It was the suckiest way ever to say goodbye to someone she cared about. She had plenty of boyfriends in the past, but never had she shared such a level of intimacy. Leaving—

"I can't believe we made it here so fast," Anne Marie chirped. The cab door opened and cold air rushed in.

Hannah opened her eyes.

Something about stepping out onto the curb would make it all real. She didn't want to go. Will. She needed him. She was a grown woman so tied up in a man it was ridiculous.

Pull yourself together.

Forcing herself to move, she got out of the cab. Would it be like this every day? Would she have to force herself out of bed each morning after spending her nights worrying if he was safe?

"Hannah!" Will's voice boomed.

He was coming out of the airport.

She dashed toward him and he caught her.

"I thought I missed you." He squeezed her so tight she lost her breath but didn't care.

"I can't believe you're here. How did you get away?"

"Doesn't matter. I'm here. Sorry our goodbyes have to be so public."

"I don't care. I—" She glanced up at him, the words stuck in her throat.

"Come on, let's get you checked in. Besides, you aren't really dressed for this kind of cold. I know, fashion before comfort. But you're going to end up with pneumonia someday."

"You're such a fast learner." Hannah refused to let go of him, but he picked up a couple of her bags with the arm that wasn't wrapped around her.

"I've had a great teacher."

They didn't talk as she checked in at the VIP counter. While she was budget-conscious about the business, she wanted Anne Marie to have the first-class treatment on British Airways. It was a far different experience than traveling coach.

The luggage was taken care of and Will took both of her hands in his. They shared intimate gazes, trying so hard to say everything inside them with their eyes.

"Now that that's all taken care of, I'm going to head to the gate," Anne Marie said.

"I'll be there soon," Hannah promised as Will led her to a corner near the line at security.

"This isn't how I imagined we would say our good-bye." He folded both of her hands in his.

She leaned in to him. "Thank you. I don't know what you did to get here, but I'm grateful."

"The idea of you leaving without—" His mouth captured hers before he finished his sentence.

The airport was crammed with people but she didn't care. Hannah opened her mouth to his and teased his tongue with hers.

Roping her arms around his neck she held on tight, filling her soul with as much strength from Will as possible. The strength of those powerful arms, the tender looks…she wasn't sure how she would live without him.

He raised his head and stared at her as if he were trying to memorize her face. She did the same to him.

"Give me your phone," she ordered him.

He gave her a questioning look but handed it over. She held it away from them and took a picture.

They were both smiling but there was a sadness in their eyes. She texted the picture so she would have it, too.

"Remember that day I said this was all in fun and that when our time was over we would walk away?" she said. "I was wrong. I mean, we talked about it before. About us caring for one another. But…don't think I'm one of those clingy women who—" She squeezed her eyes shut. "I'm not doing this the right way."

"I love you, Hannah," Will said softly.

Did she hear him right?

"This isn't the right time and I've probably scared you. But I want you to know before we part. You've become so important to me and I've loved you from the first moment I met you. Though, it took me a little while to figure out what it was. You've brought me such comfort and made me believe there is good in the world. I'll be taking you in my heart wherever I go."

"Oh, Will." She kissed him hard, giving him every piece of her heart that she could.

He loved her. Tears dropped to her cheeks and Will pulled away.

"I didn't want to make you cry."

"You didn't. I'm so happy it's spilling out of my face."

He chuckled. "I don't want to let you go but you're going to miss your flight."

"They have more flights. I can take one tomorrow."

Will frowned. "We're being deployed tonight."

"Oh, no. But the summit isn't over." Somehow if she left him in New York, she felt he was safe.

"That's the thing about being a marine, everything can change in a heartbeat."

"Do you know where?"

"Yes, but—"

"You can't say." She sighed and then gave him a bright smile. She wouldn't make him feel worse. He'd done so much for her and she wanted him to see her smiling.

"You're such a fast learner."

"I've had a great teacher."

"I'll email you daily if I can. And I'll let you know when we can chat online. Though, the hours may be squirrelly."

She choked back tears and forced a smile. "Anytime. I mean it. There isn't anything I'll want to do more than talk to you. Except maybe kiss you."

She kissed him again. Then she stepped away. "You better come home to me, Will Hughes, or I will hunt you down. Do you understand me?"

He gave her a quick salute. "Yes, ma'am."

"I want you to know that I'm going to go now and it's the hardest thing I've ever had to do in my life. But I'm going to be a grown-up if it kills me."

Taking her in his arms he kissed her again, this one lasting a full minute. "I needed to fill up my soul with you, Hannah. And know this is just as hard for me."

She walked away from him, taking shallow breaths to try to steady her emotions.

She made it through the other side of security before she realized something.

Oh, no. I never told him I loved him, too.

20

Six months later

Paris. This was her dream and she couldn't believe it had come true. After her success earlier in the year in London and New York, she'd been invited to show her new fall line as the precursor to the Jacques Le Vien show. It was an honor, and more than ever she felt the pressure to succeed.

Anne Marie snapped her fingers in front of Hannah's face. "Boss, we have a problem."

"Anne Marie, I told you. No problems tonight. We've been through everything. All the models are here. I just checked."

"It's nothing major but I need your help. Charles in the lighting booth says he has two different scripts to follow and he doesn't know which one is the right one since we changed everything up during rehearsal. I've got to get the models lined up. I'd send Jesse, but he wasn't at rehearsal. I want to make sure they get it right."

"I'm on it."

Hannah moved around the back of the stage and up to the stairway that led to the balcony where the lighting and stage crews had set up.

"Hey, guys, I heard there was some confusion."

Charles held up two scripts. "I'm not sure which one you want."

She flipped through the pages. The first one was the draft they'd devised at home before they actually saw the setup. "This is it," she said as she handed him the right one.

Kayleigh, who had been promoted to event producer, climbed into the booth.

"What are you doing up here?" Kayleigh took her seat next to Charles. "Three minutes until start time."

"Have I mentioned how much I appreciate the job you've done here? I can't believe who is sitting in that audience." Kayleigh had persuaded all of the top fashion editors and store buyers to attend.

Kayleigh waved her away. "Flattery is always welcome but we have zee show to do. So you will go and be pretty somewhere else," she said in a fake French accent.

Hannah's comm crackled. "Hey, boss," Anne Marie said, "why don't you stay out front and watch the show? We've got everything covered. Promise. It's Paris—you should see your own show."

She started to argue but Anne Marie had a point. "What about the last-minute adjustments?" Hannah was always making changes and every design that walked out on stage had to be nothing short of perfection.

"What, you don't trust me?" Anne Marie didn't sound angry but there was a tone to her voice.

"Of course I do, but this is—" She stopped herself. While she'd learned that she couldn't shove work on everyone else, there were times when she needed to give those around her more responsibilities. Will had called it raising the stakes and believed that most people rise to the occasion. "Fine, I'll stay out here a while. But make sure all the belts are centered and that Cheri wears the sapphire scarf with the blue Louboutins."

"Got it. And don't worry. We've done this one twice already in New York and London. I think we've got it down. Enjoy the show," Anne Marie said.

Hannah peered over the balcony. She couldn't believe the faces she saw below. Many of the audience members were her idols. Some of the top designers and many of her friends had arrived to show their support for her. And she had just the right amount of celebrity turnout that would give her coverage on the entertainment television shows and magazines.

"Kayleigh, you've done an amazing job with all of this. I think you managed to get everyone on my dream list."

"You hire the best, you get the best," Kayleigh said as she put her headphones on.

Hannah turned to go down the stairs. She wasn't sure she could handle being out front. If something weren't perfect she would only have herself to blame. But she changed her mind at the last minute. The gang backstage could handle the models and they were every bit as invested in the show as she was. She moved away from the booth area and sat down in the church balcony as the lights dimmed.

This was her largest collection and she'd pushed herself harder than ever. There were a couple of pieces that were risks, but she was pleased with them. Ultimately, that was all that mattered. While it was important that other people liked her designs, she created works that fed her soul. Her hope was that if she loved her creations others would, too.

The only sad note was the man she loved the most wasn't here to share it with her. They had been video chatting as much as possible, and every time she saw his face, she fell a little harder for him. But it had been more than two weeks since she'd last talked to him. He'd been sent on a special mission and she'd received an email that he would be out of touch for a while. Still, she couldn't help but worry.

She glanced up to the heavens. Praying had become almost an hourly routine. Every time he crossed her mind, she took a moment.

Please look after him. He's the only man for me and if I lose him, I don't know what I'll do.

The house lights went down and stagelights flared to life. Will's music filled the church, a mixture of rock and blues. She'd gotten the music from Dickey, who had recorded Will that night with Master Z. It had been a huge hit with the New York and London crowds. Everyone wanted to know who Will was. He'd chew her out if he knew, but it was another way to keep him close to her. Besides, the bluesy music fit the show so well.

Hannah saw people lean in to one another and imagined they were asking who that was. It was music that went straight to the soul.

Monique, one of her favorite models, stepped out in the aquamarine blouse with black wide-legged trousers and Hannah had to remind herself to breathe. The editors were madly writing in their notebooks and many of them took photos with their cell phones as Monique made her way down the carpeted runway.

As each design came out onto the stage, Hannah found herself watching the audience's faces. People were smiling. She'd been to hundreds of shows and she knew that wasn't the norm. They seemed to be genuinely enjoying the show. Of course, one never knew for sure in this business.

There was a collective gasp and her eyes shot to the stage. Hannah's breath caught.

The model had crutches under his arm, but there was no denying the hot body under the unbuttoned shirt with the low-hung jeans she'd designed just for him.

"Will." She murmured as she ran down the stairs, which wasn't an easy task in the four-inch heels she wore. By the time she ran up the side entrance of the stage he'd made his way back down the runway.

She threw her arms around him and kissed him hard on the mouth, nearly knocking them both down.

Will pulled her closer and steadied them.

Hannah was vaguely aware of the roar of the crowd

around them, then the models coming out and doing their final run.

"Is it really you?" Hannah whispered against his lips.

"Yes." He kissed her again.

Hannah's heart raced and her mind tried to wrap around the fact he really was right here with her.

"Hey, you have a show to finish. Turn around and look at those nasty fashion folks and smile like you own the world, babe."

Hannah tore her eyes away from his face to glance out. The lights kept her from seeing much but there were tears on many of the faces of those on the front row. Those hard-core editors who seldom had a nice word were clapping wildly. They weren't so nasty when they were staring at true love.

Hannah managed a smile and a quick wave.

"I think that's more for you." Hannah put a hand on his shoulder and smiled out to the audience again. "I put that you were my inspiration for the collection in tonight's program."

She'd also used the photo she'd taken at the airport. It went well with her Casablanca-themed collection.

"And you used my music." He grinned.

"Yes. You can sue me someday but not right now, okay?"

"I'd scoop you up and run for the nearest place we could be alone, but I have a feeling some of those people are going to want to talk to you."

"I don't care," Hannah said honestly. "Let's go."

He chuckled and leaned down to kiss her again. The

audience went wild. "Maybe we should at least get off the stage," he suggested.

As they moved behind the curtain Will was ambushed by their friends. Anne Marie was sobbing. "Leland told everyone about Will. They're going nuts out there. That was the most romantic thing I've ever seen," she said.

"You knew about this?" Hannah couldn't believe Anne Marie had kept a secret. That wasn't usually one of her best attributes.

"I called her about two hours ago. I wasn't sure I'd be here in time for the show. They wouldn't let me out of the damn hospital in Germany."

His words finally hit her. The crutches. "Oh, Will, you need to sit down. Are you okay? What happened? Do you hurt?"

He laughed again. "I'm fine. I'll tell you all about it later."

Well-wishers inundated them and Hannah forced herself to smile and shake hands. She didn't have any idea if they were happy about the show or about the public display of affection and she didn't care.

Hannah wasn't sure what she said to the press. Will stood next to her, fielding as many questions. After about a half hour Anne Marie shooed everyone away and Hannah was never so grateful for her friend's protective nature.

"Will. Oh, no. I've done it again."

"Hey, Hannah, what's wrong?"

She led him to a table he could sit on. She was so worried about his leg. "If the general sees this, he's going to be furious. The paparazzi loved you and your picture is going to be splattered all over the world."

Will shoved himself onto the table. He pulled her in front of him so that she was between his legs.

She tried to pull away. "I don't want to hurt your leg."

"You aren't." He wrapped his arms around her. "And you don't have to worry about the general anymore. Well, except the fact that he's always going to be my dad."

"What?"

"I've been honorably discharged." He pointed to his leg. "A sniper bullet cut my time a little shorter than I planned."

"Sniper?" A hitch caught in Hannah's throat. The possibility that he might not come back had always been in the back of her mind, but this made it so much more real.

"Yep. He was in a tower where we were trying to evacuate some kids after they found a bomb near one of the schools. Hit an artery and I would have bled out if we hadn't had medics with us who were so close by."

Her vision blurred and Hannah's mind went hazy.

"Hannah?" Will's hands tightened around her and he shifted her so that she was sitting on his good leg. She was vaguely aware of all this but she couldn't pull herself together.

"A sniper?" she said again weakly.

"Hey, I'm okay. And trust me he got one shot off and Rafe and the team took him down. I'm fine—I promise."

"You could have died." She couldn't keep the tears from falling.

"But I didn't, honey. Please stop crying. It kills me when you do that."

He thumbed her tears away.

"Will." No longer able to contain all the worry and fear she'd kept hidden from him the past few months, she sobbed against his chest.

Will rubbed her back and kissed the top of her head as he tried to soothe her.

It took her several minutes but it occurred to her she was only making things worse. "I'm sorry." She coughed. "I promised I wouldn't do that to you. I—I've been really worried. I guess I was holding more back than I thought." She gave him a half smile.

He kissed her again. This was something she would never grow tired of as long as she lived. The contact sent delightful shivers to her toes.

She pulled back. "Wait, you're not a marine anymore?"

"I'll always be a marine, but I'm no longer on active duty. I could have stayed in and done a desk job. But after watching you, I've decided to go after my own dreams. I have a way to continue to serve my country, and stay close to you."

"Tell me." She couldn't keep the anxious tone from her voice.

"Private security. Rafe and I are going into business together. We'll be private contractors with the United Nations, and thanks to Ambassador Ramkin we already have a list of clients lined up. It will mean a lot of travel, but New York is going to be home base."

"You gave up the Marines to be with me? That's— Are you sure? I don't want to be the kind of woman who forces the man she loves to give up on his dreams."

He smiled. "I love you, too."

She realized what she'd said. Every time they'd talked on the video chat she'd regretted not telling him that she loved him. But she wanted to wait until they were face-to-face again. Evidently, her subconscious was in a hurry to get the words out.

"I've loved you since that first day," she admitted. "That moment I looked into your eyes and you smiled. That was it. You owned my heart."

Will laughed. "Why did you make me work so hard, then? You knew I loved you."

She shrugged. "I was afraid you were going to leave me. It was inevitable and I think I believed if I didn't say it out loud it wasn't real. That way if you changed your mind, it wouldn't hurt so bad."

"Hannah, you are a crazy woman if you think you're ever going to get rid of me. You said something about me giving up my dreams. *You* are my dream, woman. I'd do anything to be with you. And honestly, I'm not giving up my career. I'm just taking a different path."

"So, are you rested up?" She pointed down at his leg.

"Sure, do we need to head out to some parties? I'll have to change. And I wanted to double-check to make sure all of your designs were packed and secure."

She smiled. "Anne Marie has it covered. Trust me. After the New York show, she's a fiend about making sure everything is sealed tight and locked in the crates. She's hired extra security for every show.

"And as for the parties, well, I do have something in mind." She stood and backed away from him. "But you'll have to follow me if you want to find out what it is."

"Let me get this straight. You want me to blindly follow you, wherever you go?"

She gave him a naughty grin.

"Oh, hell, yeah." He laughed as he pushed himself up on the crutches.

THE TAXI DROPPED THEM in front of a residence and Will was curious as to who they were visiting. From the look in Hannah's eyes he thought for sure they were headed back to the hotel.

"Who lives here?"

"Me. At least for now," Hannah said. "It belongs to my friend Maurice. He and his partner, Gregory, are in Italy on vacation for the next month. He knew I'd be here so he asked me to house-sit."

She opened the door and he hobbled up the steps. He hated that he was on crutches, but then he wouldn't be here if it weren't for the accident, so there was that.

When he'd seen her run up on that stage he knew he'd made the right decision. Not that he'd ever doubted his leaving the corps was the right thing to do. He couldn't lead his men the way he'd been trained with his leg the way it was. He could have stayed, but this was the second time he'd been shot in a year. He took it as a sign that it was time to go.

Hannah turned on the lights.

"What does this Maurice do?" He took in the opulence surrounding him. Everything had a distinct French feel with the gold trim and rich fabrics. While his unit would have been mortified to know it, Will had spent a great deal of time studying fabrics and style during their downtime. He wanted to better understand Hannah's world.

They passed by a painting that had been signed by Picasso.

"He's an interior designer and he has his own line of furniture that is sold around the world."

The furniture business must have been pretty good if her friend could afford something like this. Will followed her through the living and dining area into the kitchen. It was stone and steel, but still had the warmth and opulence of the rest of the place.

"You have some great friends. Do you have the whole place to yourself?"

"Usually. The staff come and go."

"That's convenient."

She waggled her eyebrows and he couldn't help but laugh.

"Are you hungry?" She opened the fridge and pulled out a bottle of champagne. Then she reached in a cabinet for a couple of glasses. When she lifted up the top of the dress tightened against her chest.

Yes, he was hungry, but not in the way she meant.

He had dreamed of her every night. Her beautiful face had replaced the horrific nightmares from his past. "Are *you* hungry?"

She shrugged. "I'm still hyper from seeing you. But I want to make sure you have your strength up." She glanced at his leg and frowned. "Oh. I… Can you… Uh…"

"Where's the bedroom?"

"It's up the stairs. Oh—"

"I'll be fine." He hoped. He turned and moved toward the staircase.

A sheen of sweat wetted his brow as he made it to the top. The pain was tough but he was a marine. He would never let it show. Hannah was behind him, and he limped onto the landing.

She moved around him to guide him to her bedroom, but when she glanced up she must have seen through the mask he'd donned.

"You need to get horizontal now," she ordered.

"I thought that was the plan."

"Not now, Marine. I knew going up those stairs would be hard for you. Stop being Mr. Tough Guy and let me help you." She handed him the other crutch she'd carried.

"I'm fine." Will hated that his breath came out in a pant. Except for his leg, he was in the best shape of his life. He'd spent a lot of time working out. Every time he talked with Hannah or read an email, it was the only way he could get rid of his sexual frustration and ease the ache in his heart.

In the bedroom, she ran to pull back the duvet and sheets. He settled back on some pillows she placed against the ornate wooden headboard. Once the pressure was off his leg, he was instantly better.

She opened the French doors looking out over Paris. It was a beautiful sight, but his eyes were focused on one woman.

"Hannah. Sit."

But she remained where she was.

"Please?" he asked her.

"I'll be back."

When she returned a minute later, she was carrying a bottle of champagne and two glasses. She uncorked the bottle and poured champagne into their glasses and handed him one. "I always think of you as being so invincible," she said softly. "If that sniper—"

She couldn't finish her sentence.

"Oh, Hannah. I promise you I'm okay. The plane ride and being up on the leg so much, that's all that's wrong. I was a little tired going up the stairs, but I'm good now." He took their glasses and set them on the nightstand. Then he nestled her against his chest. "You're always talking about the universe. The way I see it, that sniper's bullet brought me home faster to you. And he didn't hit anyone else. I considered that a win. We're here together. Nothing else matters."

She sighed against him. "It still doesn't feel real. I'm afraid I'll wake up and you'll be gone."

Gently holding her face in his hands, he kissed her. "I'm real and you just had another amazing show. I've been reading about you online. You are quite the star now. I'm so proud of you."

Hannah rolled her eyes. "Will, you were shot. What I do, it doesn't matter in the grand scheme of things. It's fluff and puff. Nothing more."

"No, babe, it isn't. What you do is art. You make beautiful clothes that make people happy. You touch lives and make people feel good about themselves. Don't you ever belittle yourself. By the way, my mom wants to know if she gets a discount."

Hannah laughed and this time it was for real. That grin of hers made Will's soul lighter.

"I don't know. It depends on how nice her son is to me." She pursed her lips as if she were thinking about something serious.

"I'm ready to be real nice to you, Hannah." His hand moved down her side.

"We can't do this. Not now," she complained. "Your leg. No."

"Oh, we can and we will."

Will picked her up and sat her on his lap.

"We should wait," she protested as he slipped her frilly dress over her head. One glance at her lacy burgundy bra and panties, and his promise to himself to take it slow was gone out the window and flying over Paris. He'd never wanted another woman so badly.

"Hannah." His thumbs rubbed across her taut nipples and she moaned.

Rubbing her heat against his hardened shaft caused his body to go rigid. If they weren't careful, he'd never make it.

"Take off your panties."

"Why, Captain Hughes, was that an order?" She stood, sliding the tiny piece of lace down to her ankles. Then she reached around and lost the bra.

Will sucked in a breath.

"You're so gorgeous."

She kneeled above him, working his zipper open and freeing his cock. Then she took him in her mouth and Will nearly lost all control. As if she had all the time in the world, she suckled him and teased him with her mouth.

"Babe, you have to stop doing that. I can't hold on much longer."

She lifted her head enough to give him a wicked glance. "Oh, no. I've been waiting months to do this, and though it's going to happen much faster than I wanted, I'm making love to you." She pulled herself on top of him. Then she leaned forward and put her hands on the headboard so they were chest to chest.

He bent his good leg so he could lift his hips to meet her, but she slid herself down on his cock and bounced on top of him, doing most of the work. Her breasts rubbed against him and her eyes bore into his with such passion.

"You think you've dreamed about this, Will? I've needed you inside me. Beside me. I love you so much and my heart left when you did. I hoped every day you would bring it home to me safe and sound." Her voice was husky with emotion.

"Technically, you were the one who left me at the airport. Though, I'm glad you had the strength to because I didn't right then."

"I'm never doing that again." Hannah increased her speed and cried out, her orgasm shuddering through her body and her slick heat tightening around his cock.

Unable to hold back any longer he spilled himself into her.

She was limp against his chest. "I love you so much, Will. I forgot to say it at the airport and I've been so mad at myself. I love you. I love you. I love you. And I'm going to spend every moment I have with you making sure you know it."

"I love you, too." He kissed the top of her head.

The woman he loved was wrapped around him and all was well with the world. For the first time in his life Will didn't care what their next move was. As long as Hannah was with him, he would be happy.

"Will?" She glanced up at him with a mischievous glint in her eyes.

"What are you thinking now?"

"Well. Since you aren't a marine anymore, maybe you could model for me."

He sighed. "I'll always be a marine. And I told you, no more modeling."

"But I was thinking it would be a private viewing. You are my muse, you know. I find the idea of dressing you up and then stripping you down extremely appealing." Her hand slid down his abdomen.

"Well, why didn't you say so? I'll model for you anytime. Here, let me show you my moves." He moved his hands behind him in a silly pose.

She laughed as she grabbed his hands. "Life will never be boring." She kissed his fingers.

"Roger that." He squeezed her hands in his. He'd thought he'd wanted a calm and quiet life. But now he knew this was the woman for him.

"Have I told you I love you?" he asked.

She gave him a sweet smile. "I think it's been close to a minute and a half since you said it last. You're slipping."

"Hmm." He pulled her on top of him. "Well, then, let me make it up to you."

* * * * *

PASSION

For a spicier, decidedly hotter read—
these are your destination for romances!

COMING NEXT MONTH
AVAILABLE NOVEMBER 22, 2011

#651 MERRY CHRISTMAS, BABY
Vicki Lewis Thompson,
Jennifer LaBrecque,
Rhonda Nelson

#652 RED-HOT SANTA
Uniformly Hot!
Tori Carrington

#653 THE MIGHTY QUINNS: KELLAN
The Mighty Quinns
Kate Hoffmann

#654 IT HAPPENED ONE CHRISTMAS
The Wrong Bed
Leslie Kelly

#655 SEXY SILENT NIGHTS
Forbidden Fantasies
Cara Summers

#656 SEX, LIES, AND MISTLETOE
Undercover Operatives
Tawny Weber

REQUEST YOUR FREE BOOKS!
2 FREE NOVELS PLUS 2 FREE GIFTS!

Harlequin Blaze

red-hot reads!

YES! Please send me 2 FREE Harlequin® Blaze™ novels and my 2 FREE gifts (gifts are worth about $10). After receiving them, if I don't wish to receive any more books, I can return the shipping statement marked "cancel." If I don't cancel, I will receive 6 brand-new novels every month and be billed just $4.49 per book in the U.S. or $4.96 per book in Canada. That's a saving of at least 14% off the cover price. It's quite a bargain. Shipping and handling is just 50¢ per book in the U.S. and 75¢ per book in Canada.* I understand that accepting the 2 free books and gifts places me under no obligation to buy anything. I can always return a shipment and cancel at any time. Even if I never buy another book, the two free books and gifts are mine to keep forever.

151/351 HDN FEQE

Name _____ (PLEASE PRINT) _____

Address _____ Apt. # _____

City _____ State/Prov. _____ Zip/Postal Code _____

Signature (if under 18, a parent or guardian must sign) _____

Mail to the Reader Service:
IN U.S.A.: P.O. Box 1867, Buffalo, NY 14240-1867
IN CANADA: P.O. Box 609, Fort Erie, Ontario L2A 5X3

Not valid for current subscribers to Harlequin Blaze books.

Want to try two free books from another line?
Call 1-800-873-8635 or visit www.ReaderService.com.

* Terms and prices subject to change without notice. Prices do not include applicable taxes. Sales tax applicable in N.Y. Canadian residents will be charged applicable taxes. Offer not valid in Quebec. This offer is limited to one order per household. All orders subject to credit approval. Credit or debit balances in a customer's account(s) may be offset by any other outstanding balance owed by or to the customer. Please allow 4 to 6 weeks for delivery. Offer available while quantities last.

Your Privacy—The Reader Service is committed to protecting your privacy. Our Privacy Policy is available online at www.ReaderService.com or upon request from the Reader Service.

We make a portion of our mailing list available to reputable third parties that offer products we believe may interest you. If you prefer that we not exchange your name with third parties, or if you wish to clarify or modify your communication preferences, please visit us at www.ReaderService.com/consumerschoice or write to us at Reader Service Preference Service, P.O. Box 9062, Buffalo, NY 14269. Include your complete name and address.

HB11B

Lucy Flemming and Ross Mitchell shared a magical,
sexy Christmas weekend together six years ago.
This Christmas, history may repeat itself when they find
themselves stranded in a major snowstorm…
and alone at last.

Read on for a sneak peek from
IT HAPPENED ONE CHRISTMAS
by Leslie Kelly.

Available December 2011, only from Harlequin® Blaze™.

EYEING THE GRAY, THICK SKY through the expansive wall of windows, Lucy began to pack up her photography gear. The Christmas party was winding down, only a dozen or so people remaining on this floor, which had been transformed from cubicles and meeting rooms to a holiday funland. She smiled at those nearest to her, then, seeing the glances at her silly elf hat, she reached up to tug it off her head.

Before she could do it, however, she heard a voice. A deep, male voice—smooth and sexy, and so not Santa's.

"I appreciate you filling in on such short notice. I've heard you do a terrific job."

Lucy didn't turn around, letting her brain process what she was hearing. Her whole body had stiffened, the hairs on the back of her neck standing up, her skin tightening into tiny goose bumps. Because that voice sounded so familiar. *Impossibly* familiar.

It can't be.

"It sounds like the kids had a great time."

Unable to stop herself, Lucy began to turn around, wondering if her ears—and all her other senses—were deceiving her. After all, six years was a long time, the mind could play tricks. What were the odds that she'd bump into *him,* here? And today of all days. December 23.

Six years exactly. Was that really possible?

One look—and the accompanying frantic thudding of her heart—and she knew her ears and brain were working just fine. Because it was *him.*

"Oh, my God," he whispered, shocked, frozen, staring as thoroughly as she was. "Lucy?"

She nodded slowly, not taking her eyes off him, wondering why the years had made him even more attractive than ever. It didn't seem fair. Not when she'd spent the past six years thinking he must have started losing that thick, golden-brown hair, or added a spare tire to that trim, muscular form.

No.

The man was gorgeous. Truly, without-a-doubt, mouthwateringly handsome, every bit as hot as he'd been the first time she'd laid eyes on him. She'd been twenty-two, he one year older.

They'd shared an amazing holiday season.

And had never seen one another again.

Until now.

Find out what happens in
IT HAPPENED ONE CHRISTMAS
by Leslie Kelly.
Available December 2011, only from Harlequin® Blaze™